.

RISEN FROM THE DEAD

A Detective Lee Burton Novel

DONALD L. ROST

RISEN FROM THE DEAD
A Detective Lee Burton Novel

Cover design by Donald L. Rost

ISBN: 979-8-9909194-0-2

This book is for my two beautiful, blonde cousins,

Leann and Robin.

"For he will order his angels
to protect you wherever you go."

Psalm 91:11

THE MYSTERIOUS VISIT

Chapter 1

Detective Lee Burton was sitting in his car at a warehouse on the west side of Phoenix, Arizona. According to his C I a drug deal was going to go down at seven p.m. Detective Burton was finishing off the last of his black coffee when all hell broke loose.

The warehouse erupted in gunfire.

He couldn't wait for back up.

Detective Lee Burton violently swung the door to his Crown Vic open. He jumped out of his car and ran toward the warehouse. He entered through a side door. By that time drug dealers and drug buyers had shot it out. By the time Detective Burton had reached the location of the melee, it was all over.

Only the drug dealers had survived the gun battle. When the gang of criminals noticed Detective Burton they all turned to him and opened fire on him. He returned fire from his service weapon then ducked behind some wooden creates. He raised up to fire again but the drug dealers fired first. An enormous amount of bullets flew in his direction.

Detective Burton went down.

The drug dealers ran to check him out. Upon noticing that he had five bullet holes in his chest, they left him for dead.

About fifteen minutes after the drug dealers had left the warehouse, his back up had arrived. They drove up with sirens blaring and lights flashing.

They ran into the warehouse and found Detective Burton lying on the concrete floor in a pool of blood.

They feared the worst.

They immediately called for an ambulance.

Within ten minutes an ambulance with siren blasting and lights flashing pulled up to the side door of the warehouse. The EMT's jumped out and ran to the back of the ambulance. They ran to the back doors and took a gurney out and ran into the warehouse. They did everything they could for Detective Burton on site, and then they loaded him into the back of the ambulance.

"I'll drive ahead of you guys and clear the road," Detective White said. "I'm guessing he needs every second he can get."

"You got that right," one of the EMT's replied.

"Where are you guys taking him?" Detective White asked..

"Phoenix Memorial."

Detective White jumped in his car and got in front of the ambulance. His tires screamed as he roared off. His siren whaled and his lights were flashing.

The ambulance sped off to catch up with him. It was a fourteen minute drive from the warehouse to Phoenix Memorial Hospital.

When the ambulance arrived at Phoenix Memorial Hospital a team of doctors and nurses were already waiting outside.

The EMT's rushed Detective Burton inside.

The doctors and nurses were doing everything they could for Detective Burton as they all hurried him inside the hospital.

They took him immediately to a waiting OR. They banged the doors to the OR open with the foot of the gurney. Everyone was running frantically into the OR.

Machines were hooked up to him.

Tubes were inserted.

Detective Burton's fellow detectives were in the waiting room. None of them would leave until they got word on how he was doing.

Doctors and nurses were working feverishly trying to save his life.

The cops were in the waiting room praying for their friend.

The doctors were doing everything possible for Detective Burton.

His friends were waiting for any little bit of information on his condition.

Ten minutes into the operation Detective Lee Burton died from his gunshot wounds.

"Okay let's call it."

"Time of death 8:03 p.m."

"Should we notify the cops in the waiting room doctor?" One of the nurses asked sadly.

"No. Let's get him cleaned up first," one of the doctors replied. "They will want to see him. I don't want them to see him covered in blood."

"Okay doctor."

Chapter 2

This all looked very strange to Detective Burton, who was floating above the operating table watching the whole thing.

Then he felt himself being pulled up. He was being pulled up through the ceiling. He felt this very peaceful feeling come over him as he was being pulled through massive amounts of white and gray clouds, and into the most brilliant light.

It all happened in a matter of seconds. He was standing in the most beautiful and colorful place he had ever seen before.

From out of the brightness walked a woman with the most perfect figure and body. She had long flowing blonde hair. She was the most gorgeous woman he had ever seen in his entire life. She slowly walked up to him as if she was floating.

"Welcome Lee," she said.

Detective Burton was totally awe stricken.

"I know this is a lot for you to take in Lee. There are some things I must tell you," she said very softly.

"Okay. Am I dead? Are you an angel?

"No. Of course not. You are not dead. And yes I am an angel."

"Then this must be heaven."

"Yes this is heaven," the angel answered.

"But why am I here angel? I have killed people."

"Yes you have. But you never did it with any malice or forethought. And that can be forgiven. You only killed to protect yourself or another person. To answer your question more about being dead. That is a misconception that a lot earth bound souls have. I am sure you have heard the phrase immortal soul before."

"Yes I have."

"What does that mean to you?" The angel asked.

"It means it lasts forever. Right?"

"Yes that is right. And it means something immortal will never die. You see Lee your soul is the real you. You just use the body until it is your time to come back home. Earth bound souls use the term die, but it only refers to the body. And no, you do not die and come to heaven and become an angel. That is another misconception some earth bound souls have. You still remain the same soul. Angels are celestial beings created by God to watch over his other souls. Unlike you, we have never lived a life on earth. Of course we can take a human form for a while to help someone who might have otherwise died before his time. But when it is your time for your earth body to die, we can not intervene."

Then Detective Burton said, "I have a question."

"Okay," the angel said. "I will let you ask it."

"Why do you always answer my questions before I ask them?"

"It is because I can read your thoughts," the beautiful angel answered. "Whenever you come back here to stay you will be able to do that too. All souls will. It is a big part of how we communicate without speaking."

"Okay," Detective Burton answered. "Why don't you have wings?"

"I do have wings. I just thought it would be more comfortable for you to see me as an earthly woman."

"Yeah, you're probably right."

"When you come back home I will answer all of your questions. But for now I must tell you why I brought here," the beautiful angel told Detective Burton.

"Okay," Detective Burton answered softly.

"You are doing a great job as a policeman. You are serving and protecting other earth bound souls who need your help. God wants you to go back to earth and continue that work. When you get the urge to quit, like you sometimes do, just remember you are doing what God wants you to do. Right now there are angels around your earth body. They are enhancing it for you. Your soul will remain the same. But they are going to make your body twice as strong as it is now. No. You will not be bulletproof. But if you do get shot the bullet will only go one inch into your body and cause no real damage. Yes you will feel it so you will know you have been injured, but it will not hurt near as bad as before."

"Cool."

"Yes it is, as you say, cool," the angel said. "When I send you back to earth, only four minutes will have past. Here we do not have time like on earth."

"But what if I want to stay here angel?"

"Most souls do Lee. But I have already explained what must happen. It is God's will."

"Yeah I know. And I am good with that."

Then the beautiful angel's voice said to Detective Burton, "Lee there is something you must do after I return your soul to your body."

"Sure anything you say."

"In three months, after your body has healed, you will be put back on active duty. Your first job will be to protect a young girl almost eighteen years old."

"I'm sorry to interrupt angel, but I am a homicide detective."

"Do not worry. We will arrange everything."

"Of course you will."

"As I was saying," the angel continued. "The young girl will witness a murder in Chicago, Illinois. She goes to the police to testify against the man that she clearly saw shoot the other man. It is a mob hit and they want the girl dead. You must protect her. She is a remarkable girl who will go on to do great things for the world."

"What does this girl do angel?"

Then the beautiful angel said to Detective Burton, "In nine of your earth years from now, there will be a terrible thing unleashed on the earth. There will be a dangerous virus originating in China. It will be very contagious. It will spread around the whole world. Many people will die. By that time this young girl will be an established doctor doing medical research. She will be the one who discovers the vaccine that will stop the virus and cure people. She must not die before her time. You must protect her at all cost Lee."

"I will protect her with my life," Detective Burton said to the angel.

"That is what I like about you Lee. You will do everything to save this girl and you do not even know her."

"It doesn't matter. It's my job. But you said she is in Chicago, Illinois. I live in Arizona."

"I know that Lee. I brought you here from Arizona. Do not worry. We will arrange it."

"Wow. You angels can do anything you want to. It's a good thing you're all good. Well you know, except for that one angel."

"Yes I do know Lee. Do not believe everything you read in the Bible. It has been changed over the years by wicked kings to control their people."

"So you mean there isn't really a ...."

"I can not tell you anymore," the angel interrupted. "I have enjoyed my talk with you Lee. But it is time for you to go back. I will allow you to remember our entire conversation when you return to earth. Remember this Lee, those five shots you took to the chest would have killed you. So when you get back to earth and hear the nurse say, 'My God it's a miracle.' It truly is a miracle. You might want to be selective as to who you tell all of this to."

Then the angel raised her arms, and when she did Detective Burton's soul started floating back away from her.

13

Then the angel said, "wait!"

Detective Burton's soul stopped immediately. He hung there in midair.

The angel said nothing. She appeared to be listening. After a few minutes she said, "I just received a message from God. I am going back to earth with you. This is a first. I will be your new partner from the twenty third precinct where I have worked for the last five years. Angels will plant memories of me in all of the police at the twenty third precinct. You will meet me in three months. I will be known in my earth body as Leann Robins."

The angel raised her arms again and Detective Lee Burton's soul continued on his journey back to his earth body. He felt himself falling back through the soft white and gray clouds. Soaring freely through the sky. He felt the warn sunshine on his soul. He felt himself slowing down as he went through the hospital ceiling and softly landed back in his earth body.

Machines started beeping and needles started moving.

The nurse who was cleaning up Detective Burton's body was totally surprised.

She yelled out, "My God it's a miracle! He's alive!"

The doctors and nurses ran back into Detective Lee Burton's room.

"What did you do?" A doctor asked.

"Nothing. I was just cleaning the blood off of him when the machines went crazy and he started breathing."

THREE MONTHS LATER

Chapter 3

*W*hat the hell could he possibly want to see me for, I thought as I walked into my new captain's office.

His name was Gabriel Angelo. I was for some reason expecting someone of Hispanic descent. Imagine my surprise to see he was as white as the driven snow. I couldn't help but notice the beautiful young blonde woman sitting across from his desk.

"Detective Burton," the captain said. "Please sit down."

I sat down in the other chair across from his desk, next to the beautiful young blonde woman.

"Thanks captain," I said.

The captain continued, "I am talking to all of the detectives under my command. You were at your doctor's office for your appointment. I saw you come in. You are the last one I need to speak with."

"Okay. What do you need to know captain?"

"I just wanted to acquaint myself with everybody while I am taking over for Captain Moore while he recovers from his surgery."

"Okay captain. I think that is a good idea."

"This is just a little get acquainted talk. Relax Detective Burton."

"Well this is pretty much me relaxed."

"Would you like a bottle of water Detective Burton?" The captain asked.

"No thank you sir. I'm good. What is it you want to see me about?"

"Well Detective Burton, I have checked your file. You have a very good record. I am really impressed. You also have a very good arrest record, and they all hold up in court. You really have everything together."

"Thank you sir. I try."

Then the captain told me, "Now that I have met you and talked to you, I like you."

"Thank you sir. I like you too, and I'm not just saying that. I really mean it. There is something about you."

"Well that is good Detective Burton," Captain Angelo said. "There is one thing I would like to ask you before we finish up here."

"What is that sir?"

"Why do they call you angel cop?"

"Well sir," I started. "Your guess is as good as mine. But I would imagine it is because I got shot a while back and had one of those near death experiences."

"Really?" The captain asked. "Tell me about it. I would like to know what it is like."

It was then that the angel's words went through my mind.

You might want to be selective as to who you tell all of this to.

"Okay sir. It was about three months ago. I got a tip from one of my CI's. He told me about a drug deal that was going to happen at seven o'clock that evening in a warehouse on the west side of Phoenix. I got there early and was waiting for back

21

up. Then all of a sudden I heard gunfire coming from inside the warehouse. I didn't wait for back up. I ran into the warehouse and into a shit load of bullets. I guess I was lucky I only got hit five times."

"Five times," the captain said in amazement. "And you are still alive. Where did you get shot?"

"All five in the chest sir."

"Wow in the chest. You sure must have a guardian angel watching over you," the captain said smiling.

"Yes sir. I, I guess I do."

"Oh please go on," the captain said. "I am sorry for the interruption."

"Well sir I was out for the rest of the story. But the guys told me when they got to the warehouse and found me, they called an ambulance right away. At the hospital they rushed me into the OR. They told me they didn't find out until later that I had died during the surgery. They said that when the doctor came out and talked to them he told them I had died for four minutes, and then came back. They had pronounced me dead and walked away. About four minutes later a nurse was cleaning up my body so my friends could come in to see me. All of a sudden they heard her yell, 'He's alive.' So they ran back into the OR and worked on me some more."

"That is interesting," the captain said.

"Here's the interesting part captain. After they pronounced me dead, I was watching them from the ceiling. I mean I was just floating above the room. Then I felt myself being pulled up. I was pulled up through the ceiling, the clouds and the sky. I ended up in the brightest light I had ever seen before. Then something totally awesome happened."

"What? What was it?" The captain asked.

"An angel walked out of the bright light. She was beautiful. She walked up to me and said, 'Welcome Lee.' She knew who I was captain. I asked the angel if I was dead. She said no. I asked her a lot of questions and she said she couldn't tell me. She said I still had work to do on earth and I must go back. It was not my time to come home yet.

Then she raised her arms in the air and I floated back into my body. All of the machines I was still hooked up to started going off. The nurse who was cleaning up my body noticed I was breathing. She called the doctors back in, and that was that."

"That is a very interesting story Detective Burton."

"I guess that is why people call me angel cop."

"Yes it probably is Detective Burton."

"But I'm not really an angel sir."

"Well of course not," the captain replied. "Oh excuse me Detective Burton. I have been very rude. I am sorry. This young lady will be your new partner for a while. She is on loan to us from the twenty third precinct. By the way, you have been cleared for active duty. Detective Lee Burton meet Detective Leann Robins."

"Detective Robins I am very happy to meet you."

"I am happy to meet you too Detective Burton."

Then the captain said, "Detective Robins is very capable of having your back. She is intelligent and did very well on the firing range."

"I don't doubt that one bit captain."

"And as fate would have it," the captain remarked. "I have your first job together."

"Great I can't wait," I told the captain.

"Yes sir. I am anxious to get started too," Leann said excitedly.

"Okay then. I got a call from Captain Collins this morning. He is with the Chicago PD."

"Chicago?" Leann asked.

"Yes Chicago. It seems he has a young girl in protective custody. She is only three months short of being eighteen years old."

"Exactly why is she being protected?" I asked.

"She was out with her friends at a movie one night. She was walking back to her car when she heard three gun shots. She turned to see what was happening and saw a man in the street light. He had just shot another man and the girl had turned in time to see him fall to the ground. She got a real good look at shooter. He started running toward her so she got into her car and sped off. He shot up the back of her car as she drove away. His car must have been parked fairly close," Captain Angelo commented. "Because he chased her down State Street shooting at her from his driver's side window. Some motorist called 911 and the Chicago police showed up. They ran him off the road and a gun battle ensued. The hit man was shot in the left shoulder and the right leg and they took him into custody."

"I am assuming the girl is okay," I asked.

"Yes," the captain replied. "She wasn't hit."

"My God that poor girl must have been scared to death," Leann stated.

"Yes I would think so," I commented.

"Here is the real problem," the captain responded. "The Chicago cops showed her some mug shots and she picked out the guy she saw. He is a well know hit man for the Chicago mob. His name is Samuel Persefone. Ever heard of him?"

"No I can't say that I have," I answered.

"No," Leann replied. "Me either."

"So what exactly does this have to do with us?" I asked.

"The mob has connections everywhere in Chicago," Captain Angelo told me. "The Chicago cops are afraid the mob will find this girl no matter where they stash her. So they want to bring her out here until the trial."

"When is the trail?" I asked.

The captain flipped through his desk calendar and said, "a month and five days from today."

"This sure is a long way to bring her. Did they say why they wanted to bring her all the way out to Arizona?" I asked.

"Well," the captain informed me. "It seems like somebody from the department read a story in the newspaper a while back about an angel cop in Arizona. They thought you would be perfect to protect her."

"They do know I'm not really an angel don't they?" I asked.

"That I don't know."

"But captain we're homicide," Leann objected.

"Well guys look at it this way, you'll be preventing a homicide," the captain replied. "Besides it has already been arranged."

There was that phrase again, it has already been arranged.

I looked to my left at Leann. I knew she could see me out of the corner of her eye, but she looked straight ahead.

I looked back at the captain and said, "What is the girl's name that we are going to be protecting?"

"Her name is Meaghan Foster. The Chicago police informed her parents they had her in protective custody. No wait. It looks like there is only one parent, the mother. She saw her for a while, then they informed her that she could not make any contact with Meaghan after she landed in Arizona. Not even a phone call."

"Well it seems like they did pretty good in that respect," I said.

"Yeah they did all right," the captain agreed.

"So when do I and Leann have to pick her up in Chicago?" I asked.

"You don't," the captain responded. "Two Chicago detectives are going to bring her out here."

"I don't think that is such a good idea captain," I said. "The fewer people who know where she is the better."

"Yeah you are probably right," the captain replied. "But it has already been arranged.

Now I'm not one to beat a dead horse, but there was that phrase again, it has already been arranged.

"Detective Burton you and Leann will meet the detectives and Meaghan at Sky Harbor tomorrow morning at eleven o'clock."

"Great," I said.

"Here is all the information you will need," Captain Angelo said, as he handed it to Leann. "Read it carefully and get to know it well. That girl's life depends on us and how we handle her protection."

"Yes sir. We know," I answered.

"Okay," the captain said. "That will be all for now."

"Okay, I am going to show Leann where the break room is. We can get a cup of coffee and look over these papers."

"Good idea," Captain Angelo said. "Maybe after that you can show Leann around the building so she will know where to find everything."

"Okay that sounds good. I would like to."

Leann and Detective Burton went to the break room for coffee.

"Well this is it Leann. It's nothing much but the coffee is free," I told Leann, while I poured myself a cup of coffee.

"Here take this one Leann. I'll get myself another cup."

"Thank you Lee. That is very nice of you."

"You're welcome. Let's just sit down at that end of the table. That way we'll be out of the way."

"Okay," Leann replied.

Leann sat down next to me and opened up the files. She took a drink of coffee.

"This is pretty good coffee," she said with a strange look on her face.

I leaned in close to her and asked, "Have you ever had coffee before?"

She answered, "No, but it is not bad."

"Hey someday I'll take you out for a good cup of coffee. You'll like it a lot better than this stuff."

"Okay thank you Lee."

"Sure you're welcome."

Leann and Detective Burton read over the files on Meaghan Foster until they had everything about her committed to memory.

"It's almost the end of our shift," I said. "Only thirty minutes left."

"Oh good," Leann sighed. "I am really tired. Hey Lee."

"Yeah."

"When can we talk in private? There is something I have to tell you."

"Okay we'll find the time before you go home tonight."

"Okay good. We'll talk about that too."

"Hey Leann. Do you want to go get a hamburger after work?"

"Sure that sounds good. I think."

"Have you ever had a hamburger before?" I asked her.

"No. That is one of the things I have to talk to you about in private.," Leann answered, looking around making sure no one was listening.

Then I said, "it's five o'clock. Let's go eat."

"Okay good."

Leann grabbed the file on Meaghan Foster.

Detective Burton walked to the sink and poured the rest of his coffee down the drain.

Chapter 4

Detective Burton and Leann walked into the restaurant.

"Hi folks. Would you like a table or a booth?" The hostess asked.

"A booth," Detective Burton replied.

"Right this way please."

"Thank you," Detective Burton responded.

Detective Burton and Leann followed the hostess to their booth.

"Here you are. Is this okay?"

"This is fine," Detective Burton said, as they sat down.

"Here is a menu for you miss, and for you sir."

"Thank you," Leann said.

The hostess walked back to the front of the restaurant.

"When the waitress comes I'll order for both of us," Detective Burton told Leann.

"Okay that will be good."

Just that second the waitress showed up.

"Hi, I am Mallory. I will be taking care of you two tonight. Are you ready to order?"

"Yes we are," Detective Burton replied. "I like your name Mallory. I don't hear that very often."

"Thank you."

"Okay. We are both going to have a hamburger with fries, both well done with the works and two Diet Cokes."

"Okay I'll get your burgers in and bring your Diet Cokes right out."

"Thank you Mallory," Detective Burton replied.

Detective Burton and Leann talked for about twenty minutes and then Mallory brought their hamburgers out.

"Here you are," Mallory said, setting their hamburgers down on the table. "Is there anything else I can get you right now?"

"No, I think we are okay," Detective Burton said.

"Great. I'll come by to check on you from time to time. If you need anything before I get back, just give me a shout."

"Will do," Detective Burton answered.

Leann took a bite of her hamburger.

"Wow. This is really good," she said excitedly.

"I figured you might like hamburgers."

"Yeah I do."

"Good."

Then Leann asked, "Hey can I talk to you about some normal stuff while we eat?"

"Sure, of course. What do you want to talk about?"

"When I met you three months ago, you said you were a homicide detective."

"Yeah I am."

"Then why were you at a drug bust?"

"Okay. That's a fair question. I was there because one of my CI's informed me that one of the drug dealers was the guy who shot and killed my partner before you."

"Oh."

"So I got my captain to talk to the DEA captain, so I could join them on the raid. Then I could arrest my suspect. So you see it was a homicide related deal."

"Yes I do see. I just wondered because you made such a point of bringing that up when I told you about protecting Meaghan Foster."

"I wasn't bringing it up as a protest. I just didn't see how I would be able to do it, until it was all arranged."

"Okay I understand it all now," Leann told Detective Burton.

"Good."

Then Mallory came back to the table.

"Would you like refills?"

"Leann?" Detective Burton asked.

"Yes, I would like a refill."

"Yeah make it two."

"Sure I'll be right back," Mallory said, as she reached for their glasses and left.

"I hope you do not mind that I got a refill. I like it."

"I don't mind at all. I'm not in a hurry."

"Here are your refills and your check. Just take your time, and if you need anything else please let me know. I'll take that when you're ready."

"Okay thank you Mallory," Detective Burton said.

"She was nice," Leann said.

"Yes she was," Detective Burton agreed. "Just a young girl trying to make a living."

A short time later.

"Are you almost done Lee?"

"Yeah we can go. I think I have had enough to drink."

"Yes me too," Leann agreed. "Can we go to your house to talk in private?"

"Sure. Just let me pay the check."

Detective Burton turned the check over.

It was $41.42.

He reached into his pocket for some change. He left $51.42 on the table.

"Okay Leann, let's go."

"Lee?"

"Yeah."

"Why are all of those men staring at you?"

"Trust me Leann. They're not staring at me. They are staring at you. I'll explain later."

"Okay. Let's go Lee."

Chapter 5

Inside Detective Lee Burton's apartment.

"Let's sit on the couch and relax," Detective Burton told Leann.

"Okay there are some things I need to tell you," Leann replied.

"Okay, I kind of figured."

"When I was in heaven I never had to eat or drink or sleep. This is all new to me. God made this body for me. It is just like all earth women. I have all the parts and they are fully functional. I just don't have all of my angel powers. I must help you as a normal earth woman."

"Okay Leann. That's all I could ask of anyone."

"You are not disappointed?"

"Of course not. I like you just the way you are."

"Okay, but now I will have to eat and drink and sleep, just like a real earth woman."

"Leann, you are a real earth woman."

Then Leann said, "I have spent a lot of time in the last three months learning how earth women act. I just wasn't sure about the food. So will you order for me until I get the hang of it?"

"Sure. I will."

"Okay then, from now on we drop the angel references so nobody overhears us."

"Sure I got it."

Then Detective Burton said to Leann, "you want to stay and talk for a while before you go home?"

"Yes Lee. I would like that."

"I should tell you something Leann."

"What?"

"Well by earth standards, or I guess by any standards. You are a very beautiful woman. You are going to have to get used to men staring at you."

"Why?"

"Well because it's just something that men do. I do it too. You can't hit them for it or tell them off. You see you are a cop now, like me. We can't do things like that."

"I see. I have been briefed on most of earth's ways."

"Good. I think we have got it covered now."

"Okay. Do you mind if I look around your apartment?"

"No. Go right ahead."

"Thank you Lee."

"Hey Leann."

"Yes."

"Do you want me to make us some hot chocolate while you look around?"

"Yes, I will try that too."

"Just a word to the wise. If you are going to be an earth woman, you're going to have to learn to like chocolate."

"Okay I will," Leann said, as she went to look around Detective Burton's apartment.

Detective Burton went to the kitchen to make the hot chocolate.

In five minutes Leann was back.

"Oh good. You're just in time. Would you like to try these little marshmallows in yours?"

"Yes I would."

Detective Burton and Detective Leann Robins sat down at the kitchen table.

"Just go ahead and take the lid off the bowl and get some marshmallows. I keep them in a plastic bowl with a lid on it to keep them fresh longer."

"I see."

Leann took a sip of the hot chocolate.

"Oooohh, this is really good."

"Yeah I like it too. I drink it to help me sleep better."

"Does it work?"

"Not really."

"Why not?"

"I don't know. I just don't sleep much more than four hours a night, if I'm lucky."

"I know what you need Lee."

"Yeah me too," Detective Burton thought.

"No not that. Well probably. But I can't give you that."

"Boy you really have been briefed in the ways of the earth woman."

"Yes I told you I have."

"Hey wait a minute Leann. You heard me thinking, didn't you? You said you didn't have any of your angel powers."

"No. You didn't let me finish. I said I didn't have all of my angel powers. But for some odd reason I am able to read your thoughts and nobody else's."

"Great. That's just great."

"It is?" Leann asked.

"Yes it actually is. If I just think something you can hear it. Right?"

"Yes I can."

"God really thinks ahead," Detective Burton said smiling.

"What do you mean?"

"Well think about it Leann. If we get into a bad situation and I see something to get us out, like if we get caught by bad guys."

"Yes."

"I can think of something for you to do and you can hear me."

"I see where you are going with this Lee."

"Yeah this will be cool…….sometimes."

"Hey Lee."

"Yeah."

"I have to ask you something."

"Sure, anything."

"I noticed when I was looking around your apartment, you have two bedrooms."

"Yeah. Me and my other partner used to share this place."

"Can I stay here with you. I don't have any place else to go. I just got here about three hours before I met you in the captain's office."

"You mean here, on earth?"

"Yes."

"Well that's cuttin' it pretty close."

"I know. I was busy."

"You probably don't have any other clothes either. Do you?"

"No."

"Well it's only nine o'clock. Walmart is open. We need to get you two or three outfits until we have more time. Then you can go on a shopping spree. Trust me, you'll like it."

"Lee?"

"Yes."

"You didn't answer my question about staying with you tonight."

"Of course you can stay with me Leann. We're partners."

"Thank you."

"You're welcome. Let's go to Walmart."

THE NEXT DAY

Chapter 6

It was ten thirty in the morning.

Detective Lee Burton and Detective Leann Robins pulled into Sky Harbor Airport.

"We're doing good Leann. We shouldn't have to wait too long for them."

"Good."

"I'll park in this lot and we'll go in the Southwest Airlines door. We'll wait by the baggage carousel."

"But how will we know who they are Lee?"

"They're cops Leann. They can't be that hard to spot."

"Really?"

"Really. Besides there can't be that many two men and a teenage brunette groups traveling together."

"Yeah I guess you are right Lee."

After about thirty minutes Detective Burton looked at Leann when he saw two men in suits and a teenage girl with dark hair coming around the baggage carousel.

"Hey I'll bet that's probably them now." Detective Burton said.

"Yeah it could be. Let's go get them."

Detective Burton and Detective Robins walked up to the weary trio of travelers.

"Hi there," Detective Burton said. "Are you two guys the detectives from Chicago?"

"Yes we are," answered Detective Ryan. "I am Detective Ryan and he is Detective Moorehead."

"How are you doin'?" Detective Moorehead asked.

Then Detective Burton said, "We are fine. I am Detective Burton and she is my partner Detective Robins."

Then they all got their handshakes out of the way.

"You must be Meaghan," Leann said.

"Yes I am. I'm glad to meet you Detective Robins, and you too Detective Burton."

"You don't have to be so formal Meaghan. You can just call me Leann."

"Well, you're already starting off better than these two," Meaghan told Leann.

"Watch your mouth kid," Detective Ryan demanded.

"You need to calm down there Ryan," Detective Burton said. "Do I detect a little tension in your voice Meaghan?"

"No. I'm okay."

"We've got it from here," Detective Burton stated. "You guys can go."

"It's not that easy," Detective Ryan replied. "My captain wants me to stay and help you protect the kid. He wants us to still have a hold on her. You know, to make sure everything goes okay."

"Okay if that's how it has to be," Detective Burton responded. "If that is how it was arranged. I'll find out when we get back to the station and talk to my captain. If not, you'll be on the first plane out of here."

Then Detective Moorehead said to Detective Burton.

"So you're the angel cop?"

"That's what they call me. But you do know I'm not really an angel, don't you?"

"Yeah I figured you probably weren't."

"Yeah me too," Detective Ryan said. "Now Leann here looks more like she could be an angel cop."

"Watch it Ryan," Detective Burton growled. "That's a good way to get your ass kicked."

"Oh I don't know. She don't look that tough to me."

"I was talking about me. But just so you know, she could slap the piss out of you without even breaking a sweat."

By this time people in the airport were stopping to watch the two men argue.

"Come on guys. Calm down," Detective Moorehead said. "You guys are going to have to work together."

"Don't worry," Leann said. "I'll keep them apart."

"Well Detective Robins it sure was a pleasure meeting you, and you too Detective Burton. I have a plane going back to Chicago in about two hours. So I'm going to get me a good meal before I head back."

Detective Burton said, "I know a good motel right down the road, if you want to stay the night and head back in the morning."

"No. I'll just head back today yet. It's only a little under a three hour flight."

"Okay then, have a good flight back."

"Yeah have a good flight," Leann said.

"Okay you two take care. I'll see you when you get back to Chicago Ryan."

"Yeah you will."

With that Detective Moorehead walked away, in search of a good meal.

Detective Burton, Leann and Meaghan watched as the Chicago detective disappeared into the crowd.

Detective Ryan looked at Leann and said, "I could eat something."

"Yeah me too," Meaghan said.

"Okay sweetie," Leann said. "I am new to this area. But my partner Lee knows a lot of good restaurants where we can eat. What would you like to have?"

"I would like to have a big hamburger with fries."

"Good," Leann said. "I like hamburgers too."

"Are you guys ready to go eat yet?" Detective Ryan asked. "I'm starving."

Then Detective Burton asked," How much longer do you think it would take for you to starve?"

"Real funny Burton. You're a real comedian."

"Well we're sure as hell not going to eat here in this madhouse," Detective Burton informed everybody. "I know a good place on the way back to the station."

"Hey Lee, take Meaghan over to the end of the luggage carousel. I have to talk to Detective Ryan for a minute."

"Sure thing Leann," Detective Burton replied.

When Detective Burton and Meaghan were at the end of the luggage carousel, Leann turned to Detective Ryan and said, "Let's get something straight right now. I don't like your attitude and neither does Detective Burton. Let me tell you something about him. Three months ago he got permission to go on a drug raid with DEA. He was waiting for the rest of his team when he heard gunfire coming from within the warehouse. He went into the warehouse without back up."

"Yeah I know. I read all about him in the paper."

"Yeah. Well here is the part that wasn't in the paper. He was greatly outnumbered and was shot five times in the chest by various different guns. The rest of his team finally showed up and took him to the hospital. During the surgery he died. The doctors pronounced him dead and left the operating room. He was dead for four minutes then came back. I don't know where he went or what happened to him. But he came back different, stronger than he was before. So is he still Lee or an avenging angel. Your guess is as good as mine. But now he has absolutely no fear. He came back one bad ass man. I'm just telling you this because if you don't change your attitude I'm going to turn him loose on you. All I have to do is tell him you touched me in an inappropriate way. I don't want him to get suspended or put in jail for beating you to a pulp."

"Okay. Okay Leann. I know I can come on a little strong sometimes……."

"And another thing," Leann interrupted. "From now on you call me Detective Robins, until I tell you different. Which at this point will probably be never. And you refer to Lee as Detective Burton. You show some respect to everybody."

"Yeah. Sure," Detective Ryan stammered.

"Okay then. Let's go."

When they got to the end of the carousel.

Detective Burton asked Leann, "Was everything okay over there? You talked to him for a pretty long time."

"Yes. I was just trying to make a point. I think I might have done what you call…….OVERKILL."

Chapter 7

Thirty minutes later at the restaurant.

"You can just seat yourselves. Where ever you would like to sit," a voice from behind the counter said.

"Oh cool. Can we sit over there by the window?" Meagan asked.

"I don't know about that," Detective Ryan replied.

"The window is fine Meaghan," Detective Burton said. "Find a table you like."

"Thanks."

"Yeah by the window is fine," Detective Ryan said.

Detective Burton, Leann and Detective Ryan followed Meaghan to the table where she wanted to sit and eat.

"Hi folks. Are you ready to order?" The waitress asked.

"Yes I think we are. Right?" Detective Burton asked.

"Yeah I'm all set," Leann gushed.

"Me too," Meaghan replied.

"I've been ready for an hour," Detective Ryan responded.

Then he felt Leann kick him under the table.

"Ooouuhh! What I meant ma'am was I just came in on a flight from Chicago and I'm pretty hungry."

"Oh okay."

"Are we all still having hamburgers all fries all the way around," Detective Burton asked.

"Yes I am," Leann answered.

"Yeah me too," Meaghan replied.

"Sure," Detective Ryan said.

"I am definitely having the hamburger and fries," Detective Burton stated.

"Okay," the waitress said. "I'll get them started for you sir."

"Okay then," Detective Burton sighed. "Before you put those hamburgers in, could you put the three of us on one check and put him on a separate check."

Chapter 8

In Captain Angelo's office.

"Hey come on in guys. How did your trip to the airport go?"

"It was okay," Detective Burton replied.

Captain Angelo said, "This must be Meaghan. How are you young lady?"

"I'm fine."

Then Detective Ryan walked in from around the corner of the wall.

"Who is that?" Captain Angelo asked.

"That is Detective Ryan," Leann answered.

"What is he doing here?" Captain Angelo asked.

"My thoughts exactly," Detective Burton responded.

"Well sir," Leann answered. "He is one of the detectives who escorted Meaghan here."

"Then why is he still here? Let him answer. Why are you still here Detective Ryan?"

"My captain wants me to stay here and be a part of the protection team. He wants someone here who can keep him informed as to what is going on."

"Oh I see," Captain Angelo replied. "Well I am not going to get in the way of that right now. But keep this in mind Detective Ryan, Detective Burton is in charge of the operation. Whatever he says you do with no questions asked. Is that clear?"

"Yes sir. That's clear."

"Okay then," Captain Angelo stated. "Take a look at these Detective Burton. We have five safe houses available right now. I want you to pick out one of these and let me know which one you have decided on."

"Yes sir. I'll do that."

"Do you mind if I look at them too?" Meaghan asked.

"Of course not honey," Leann answered. "Come right on over here at the desk with us."

"Great, Thanks Leann."

"Hey Meaghan do you swim?" Detective Burton asked.

"Yeah, I was a swimmer on my high school swim team."

Detective Burton said, "Good then. Let's pick one that has a pool. How does that sound?"

"That sounds great. I love it."

"Well good. It looks like we have two of them. Which one do you like best? Take your time. Give them a good looking over."

Meaghan looked at the two houses for a long time. She studied the inside of the house so well, in fact she looked them over so well you would think she was buying one.

Then finally she said, "I really like this one the best Detective Burton."

"You know what Meaghan, so do I. That is the one I would have picked."

"Really."

"Yeah really," Detective Burton beamed.

"That is the one I would have picked too," Leann said.

"Does anybody care what I would have picked?" Detective Ryan asked.

"No." Detective Burton and Leann said at the same time.

"Well okay then," Detective Ryan responded.

Then Detective Burton spoke up and said, "let's get one thing straight right now Ryan. You're just along for the ride. I don't want to hear your opinions. I don't want to hear your suggestions and I don't want to hear you gripe at every little thing. It's going to be hotter than hell this time of year, so get used to it. And I don't want you to get in my way. My job is to protect that little girl right there, and by God I'm going to do that at any cost. Do you understand what I mean?"

"Yeah, I got ya."

"I would suggest that you get a motel room for a couple of days Ryan. Because the safe house won't be ready for a couple of days."

"But what about the kid," Detective Ryan asked.

"Don't worry about Meaghan. Leann and I will take care of her until the safe house is ready. Then you can go there with us. Besides, nobody knows where she is. Right?"

"Yeah. Right." Detective Ryan answered.

"Okay then. Meet us here Wednesday morning at nine o'clock and we'll take off to the safe house together. Just consider it a couple of days off."

"Okay."

"Talk to the desk sergeant on your way out. He will help you find a good motel to stay in."

"Okay thanks. I'll see you Wednesday."

Detective Burton watched Detective Ryan walk to the front desk. He walked over and closed the captain's door.

"Okay Detective Burton, I let you take the lead on that," Captain Angelo said. "So what's the deal? I'm sure you know the safe houses are ready now."

"Yes I do. But that house is not ready for the way I need it. Give me the address sir."

"Sure. Here it is."

"Don't say it out loud captain. I'll just copy it down."

"Okay, here it is," Captain Angelo said as he laid the paper on the desk.

"I'll explain all of this to you later captain, before we leave for the safe house."

"Okay. I trust you with this Lee."

Then Detective Burton leaned in close to the captain and whispered, "I'm going to save the state a couple of nights of money. Leann and I are going to take Meaghan to my place while we are waiting to go to the safe house. There are a couple of things I need to do to it first."

When Detective Burton was walking away Captain Angelo said, "Lee you don't trust Detective Ryan do you?"

"I don't like him. I don't know if I don't trust him yet. After all he is a cop. I have to give him the benefit of the doubt."

"I understand Lee."

"Oh I almost forgot captain. Do you have that credit card for us?"

"Yeah I'm glad you reminded me. It's totally untraceable. There is no name on it. It's just a card loaded with three thousand dollars on it. If you need more just call me and I'll have more money loaded on it."

"I'll do that. But I'm sure it will last us for the two days we are at my house."

Detective Burton saw the look on the captain's face.

"Just kidding," he said, smiling at the captain.

"Well I hope so," Captain Angelo replied, smiling back at Detective Burton.

"Do you care if we go right now captain?" Detective Burton asked.

"Go."

"Thanks."

"Okay girls. Let's go to my place," Detective Burton said.

Leann and Meaghan followed Detective Burton out to the motor pool.

"Why are we going to the motor pool?" Leann asked.

"Because I had Chucky make up something special for us."

"I can't wait to see this," Leann stated. "I'll bet it looks like something out of those Road Warrior movies."

"Oh that would be so cool," Meaghan roared.

"Hey Chucky. You got my car ready?"

"Sure Lee. It's that one over there."

"Oh my God," Leann shrieked.

"No," Chucky said. "Not that one. The red one parked behind it."

"Oh, that is so much better," Leann replied. "I like that one, it's really cool looking."

"Yeah it sure is," Meaghan giggled.

"Okay Lee, it's all re-enforced like you asked. It's a 2011 Dodge Charger 370 Horse Power, 5 speed auto transmission, it's an 8 banger with turbo charger, the tires will grip the road and it goes from 0 to 60 yesterday."

"Chucky my man. I owe you big time."

"Okay Lee. I'll hold you to that."

"Chucky you know I'm good for it."

"I know Lee. I trust you."

"Where are the keys Chucky. We have got to go. We're burning daylight here."

"Here's the keys Lee."

"Thanks Chucky."

Detective Burton, Leann and Meaghan went out to the Charger and got in.

"Really Leann," Detective Burton said. "The Road Warrior. That would be too conspicuous. That would attract way too much attention."

Then they all laughed.

"You know Meaghan, as far as I know nobody knows where you are. I would really like to take you out somewhere to eat. But I can't really take the chance. I swore to someone that I would protect you with my life. So I think we should go to my apartment and order in."

"Sure," Meaghan said. "It's okay. I understand."

"Good," Detective Burton said. "I'll try to make it up to you when we get to the safe house."

"Okay," Meaghan said.

Chapter 9

Thirty minutes later at Detective Burton's apartment.

"Okay ladies make yourselves at home. I've got lots of stuff to drink in the fridge. I've got plenty of chips and popcorn. I'm a chip eater myself."

"Me too," Meaghan said.

"You want to try some chips with me and Meaghan later Leann?"

"Sure I'll try some chips."

"I have plenty of food too. I can cook us up some hamburgers or a chicken. But, since I did promise Meaghan we would order in tonight, what would you like to have to eat?"

"Oh gee, I'm not really sure," Meaghan sighed.

"Well maybe I can help you," Detective Burton replied. "Look in that drawer over there, the one on the far left. It has all kinds of take out menus."

Meaghan ran over to the drawer and pulled it open.

"Wow, you sure do have a lot of places to order from."

"Yeah I sure do. A lot of times I just don't feel like coming home and cooking for forty five minutes."

"Yeah I know what you mean," Leann said. "Pick something good Meaghan."

Then Detective Burton said, "I know it is still early, but when it comes time to go to bed, Leann you and Meaghan can sleep in the master bedroom and I'll take the extra bedroom. There are some clean sheets in the closet with the sliding doors out there in the hall."

"Okay Detective Burton," Meaghan replied happily.

"Good. We got that all straightened out."

"I figured out what I want to have for dinner," Meaghan said.

"Good what did you decide on?" Detective Burton asked.

"I would like to have some spaghetti with bread sticks and a salad. Is that okay with everybody else?"

"That sounds great to me," Detective Burton said.

"Sure I will try that," Leann answered.

"Good," Meaghan said. "We can order it all from this pizza place."

"All right," Detective Burton said. "Would you like to call it in Meaghan?"

"Yeah sure. I'll do it right now."

"Good," Detective Burton said. "Here use my phone. Put it on this credit card the captain gave me and tell them we will give the tip in cash when it is delivered."

Meaghan took Detective Burton's phone and credit card and sat at the table with the pizza menu spread out.

When Detective Burton saw Meaghan dialing the phone number he pulled Leann to the side.

"Hey Leann come here."

"What is it Lee?"

"I think we will be okay with Meaghan being here for a couple of days. The advantage we have here is I know this place very well in the dark. If anything does happen, I want you to take her into the bedroom and stay with her."

"Okay."

"But we should be good here."

"Okay!" Meaghan shouted. "It will be here in forty minutes. Now I am really getting hungry."

"I think we all are," Leann responded.

"Hey Meaghan," Detective Burton said. "I'll bet you sure have had a rough day. I know Leann and I have."

Yes I have Detective Burton. Especially with that asshole Ryan around."

"Yeah that is pretty much my opinion of him too."

"That other guy Detective Moorehead was all right. He was a nice guy."

"Ryan didn't hurt you did he Meaghan?" Detective Burton asked.

"No, not physically. It was just the constant verbal jabs."

Then Detective Burton said to Meaghan, "You won't have to worry about him anymore. I'll keep him away from you as much as I can."

"Thank you Detective Burton."

"Hey, why don't you call me Lee?"

"Okay I'll do that."

"Well you'd better. We're friends now, aren't we?"

"Yes we are," Meaghan answered, with a big smile on her face.

"The reason I asked you about your day in the first place, was to see if you and Leann would like to get showers. I know that always perks me up. I'll keep watch until you girls get done. But I think we are pretty safe here though."

"Okay Meaghan," Leann said. "Let's go."

Leann and Meaghan went to take their showers.

Chapter 10

D etective Burton waited patiently for Leann and Meaghan to return.

In Detective Burton's bedroom.

"I feel so much better now Leann."

"Yeah me too."

"Gosh Leann, you are so pretty."

"Thank you Meaghan. But you still have than little girl cuteness. You'll grow into pretty."

"How can you be so sure Leann?"

"You will. Trust me on that."

Back in Detective Burton's living room.

"Okay Lee," Leann said. "We are all done. Now it is your turn."

"Okay girls, I'll see you in about fifteen minutes. If the food comes before I get done, I left a ten on the end of the table. That's the tip."

"Okay," Leann replied.

Detective Burton picked his gun up from the coffee table, put it in its holster and then headed for the extra bedroom.

"Does he always take his gun with him to take a shower?" Meaghan asked.

"Meaghan you are going to see Lee do a lot of strange things while he is protecting you. He is not always like that. He takes his job very seriously. You don't have to be afraid while he is here. He will protect you with his life. That is the kind of guy he is sweetie."

"Wow, I didn't know."

"Now you do," Leann whispered.

"I really like Lee," Meaghan told Leann.

"So do I," Leann answered softly.

Chapter 11

Fifteen minutes later Detective Burton came back from taking his shower.

"Wow. You sure look good all cleaned up," Meaghan commented.

"Yes you sure do Lee," Leann agreed.

"Thank you ladies. You both look beautiful. But if I had said that first it would have been weird."

"Why?" Meaghan asked.

"Because women are a lot different today than they were twenty years ago Meaghan."

"What do you mean they're different?" Meaghan asked Detective Burton.

"Well a man used to be able to give a woman a nice compliment and flirt with her a little bit without being slapped or having a sexual harassment charge put against him."

"Yeah I have heard a lot about that," Meaghan said.

"Don't be like that Meaghan. But also learn to defend yourself, just in case it comes to that."

"Okay I got ya Lee."

"Hey," Leann said. "The food came while you were in the shower. Let's eat."

"All right let's go," Detective Burton replied.

Detective Burton, Leann and Meaghan ate and enjoyed their meal. They laughed and talked for about an hour.

When Meaghan excused herself to go to the bathroom, Detective Burton said to Leann, "I have to make a couple of phone calls tomorrow. I want to get the safe house fixed up the way I want it. I want you to keep this just between the two of us. I especially don't want Ryan to know what I am doing to it."

"Of course Lee. I will not tell a soul."

THE NEXT DAY

Chapter 12

In Detective Lee Burton's apartment.

"Well did everybody have enough breakfast?" Detective Burton asked.

"Yes, I am stuffed," Meaghan replied. "You sure are a good cook Lee."

"Yes you are," Leann said. "This was delicious."

"Thank you ladies. I appreciate the compliments."

"I am going to get another cup of coffee," Leann stated. "The coffee is really good too."

"Okay ladies," Detective Burton said. "Make yourselves at home. Get anything you want. I am going to get another cup of coffee and take it to my room. I have to make a couple of phone calls to get some stuff for the safe house. I'll be back out in a little bit."

"Okay we'll be right here," Leann responded.

Detective Lee Burton took his coffee and headed into the master bedroom. He pulled out his cell phone and laid it on the desk next to his laptop. Then he dialed the number to Grayson's Body Shop.

"Grayson's Body Shop. Grayson speaking."

"Hey Grayson it's Detective Lee Burton. How are you doing today?"

"I'm good. How are you Lee?"

"I'm okay. I got something I want you to do for me."

"Okay Lee. Just name it."

"Well I ordered one of those chests that you put at the foot of the bed, you know to put sheets and blankets and stuff in."

"Sure I know what you mean."

"Okay I ordered it from that furniture store down the road from your shop. It's Eagle Furniture Warehouse."

"Yeah I know right where it is Lee."

"Okay Grayson, I am going to email you the invoice. I already told them you would be picking it up for me. It's paid for and ready to pick up."

"Okay I can do that for you," Grayson said.

"I am also going to send you the plans I drew up for the modifications I need you to make. And it's a rush job. I need it to be ready by tomorrow morning at nine a.m. It's not that much work. I'll pay you for picking it up too."

"All right, I'll have it done for you Lee."

"Perfect. I will also send you the credit card number to use, to pay for the job and yourself for picking it up."

"Okay that's great Lee."

"Oh one more thing. I need you to load it up in one of your pickup trucks and strap it in real good. And also strap in a two wheeler for me. I'll need it for about four hours, so put the truck rental on the card too."

"Okay will do."

"Thanks Grayson. I'll see you tomorrow morning at nine o'clock."

"Okay Lee."

"Bye," Detective Burton told Grayson.

"Bye Lee."

Chapter 13

Detective Burton made one more phone call.

He dialed the number.

The phone on the other end rang.

"This is Aaron's Gun Shop. Big or small, we got 'em all. Aaron here."

"Hey Aaron, how the hell are you?"

"I'm good. How are you?"

"Doin' good."

"Hey is this Detective Burton?"

"It sure is."

"God I haven't heard from you in a coon's age."

"Well my job usually doesn't call for the heavy stuff that we don't already have."

"Yeah I know. You guys are pretty well armed for cops."

"Damn right we are. Hey Aaron I have a special job that is really important. I am going to need a few things that are not police issue, if you know what I mean."

"Oh I know what you mean. I was in combat just like you Lee. But you are the one guy I would never want to go up against."

"Let's hope you never have to."

"Hey Lee, as long as you are out there, I'm going to be good."

"That's good. Now let me tell you what I need."

"Shoot," Aaron said, with a little chuckle.

"Okay Aaron," Detective Burton went on. "I need two M-16 rifles, with six bandoliers full of ammo. I need the military bandoliers, the green cloth ones."

"Yeah I know. I can get those."

"Great. Make sure the magazines only have eighteen rounds in each one to take the tension off of the springs."

"Got it."

"I need four Claymore mines and five burner phones."

"Damn Lee. You're not planning on starting a war with some third world country are you?"

Detective Burton laughed and said, "No, I'm not going to do that. But I am preparing for trouble. Trouble that I hope never comes. I'm going to be holed up in a safe house for a while."

Then Aaron replied, "I sure would hate to be the poor bastard that comes after you."

"Yeah I know. They are going to be in for one hell of a surprise."

"I'll say."

"Aaron I hate to ask you to do something that's not in you expertise. But I am really pressed for time."

"Don't worry about it. What do you need?"

"Can you get me a tarp and wrap the M-16s, the Claymores, ammo and stuff in it. Then fold the ends over and duct tape them together. Then put some tape around the middle. I want to be able to move this stuff around without losing anything."

"Sure I can do that for you."

"Also would you pick me up four bags of Turf Builder? The five thousand square foot bag will be plenty."

"Sure I'll get that for you. But I am just a little curious as to what the hell you're going to make out of it."

"Nothing. I need something to set in front of the Claymores to hide them."

"Of course you do. You don't want them setting out in the open. A trained bad guy might spot them."

"My thoughts exactly Aaron. But if I do have to set off those Claymores, that front lawn is gonna to be greener than Shrek's ass."

"Yeah for sure."

"Hey can I pick all of that stuff up tomorrow around nine thirty or so?"

"You bet. I'll have it ready for you."

"Thanks Aaron. I got to go."

"Take care Lee."

"Yeah you too."

The next day Detective Burton went out and picked up all of his supplies and took them to the safe house. He set everything up just the way he wanted it. Then he went back to his apartment.

THE THIRD DAY AFTER MEAGHAN'S ARRIVAL IN ARIZONA

Chapter 14

Thursday morning in Captain Angelo's office.

It was nine fifteen a.m.

Detective Burton, Detective Robins and Meaghan had to act like they didn't know anything about the safe house for Detective Ryan's benefit.

Detective Lee Burton said, "Okay captain we have everything we need packed in the car and we're all ready to go."

"Good," Captain Angelo replied. "I guess all you need now is the address to the safe house."

"Yeah that's all," Detective Ryan responded.

"I can't wait to get there," Meaghan said. "Lee told me you might even give us one with a pool."

"Well what a coincidence," Captain Angelo answered. "This one does have a pool."

"Oh that's so cool," Meaghan replied excitedly.

"Yes it is," Leann said. "I might even do a little swimming myself."

"All right people," the captain said. "You need to get out to the safe house and get set up. Here is the address Detective Burton."

"Good. Thanks captain," Detective Burton answered.

"And here are the keys and the garage door opener. I assume you will be doing the driving."

"Yep that's me sir. The designated driver."

Then Captain Angelo said, "You guys be careful out there, and take care."

"We will sir," Detective Burton answered.

"Bye Captain Angelo," Leann said, with an expression on her face that only Captain Angelo saw.

Detective Burton, Detective Robins, Detective Ryan and Meaghan Foster all went out to the parking lot.

"Where is your rental car parked Ryan?" Detective Burton asked.

"That's it down on the end," Detective Ryan answered.

"So have you got your suitcase and everything else you need in it."

"Yep."

"Okay then," Detective Burton said. "I'll get the girls loaded up and drive down there. You can throw your stuff in the trunk with ours."

"All right thanks," Detective Ryan said.

"Okay girls. Let's get in the car."

"Yeah let's go," Leann replied.

"Yeah I can hardly wait to see the place," Meaghan said.

They all got into the Dodge Charger and Detective Burton drove them down to Detective Ryan's rental car.

Detective Ryan loaded his things into the trunk of the Charger and got in the front passenger's seat.

"Red?" Detective Ryan said as a question.

"Yeah. I couldn't get one in bright orange on such short notice. Besides this is a dull red."

"Oh okay."

"The bad guys would never look for us in a car like this."

"You're right Lee," Meaghan said. "They will be looking for us in a black SUV."

"Exactly," Detective Burton replied.

Detective Burton drove the Charger onto Highway101. He keep his speed at sixty MPH, so he would not draw any unnecessary attention.

Chapter 15

Forty five minutes after leaving the station Detective Burton backed the dull red Charger into the driveway of the safe house.

He opened the garage door and backed the Charger inside.

He closed the door after he turned off the engine.

"Okay here we are. Home sweet home," Detective Burton said. "Let's go in and get settled."

Everybody went inside the house and Detective Burton locked the door.

"Well I sure am glad somebody came by yesterday and turned on the air conditioner," Detective Burton stated.

"Yeah me too," Leann replied. "Especially since you two are from Chicago. You will probably want to stay out of the heat as much as you can for a while."

"Yeah," Detective Burton said. "Don't let all of that it's a dry heat crap fool you. When it's 118 degrees out, that's hot."

"Wow," Meaghan said. "If it's 118 degrees out that will be some good swimming weather."

"That is for sure," Detective Burton agreed.

"What time do you guys usually have lunch?" Leann asked, pulling open the refrigerator door. "It looks like we are pretty well stocked."

"Whenever you guys want to eat is fine with me," Detective Burton answered. "I'm going outside and check around."

"Okay," Leann said. "Just be careful Lee."

"I will. Besides nobody knows we're here except for the five of us, and for me that's two too many. But we'll see how things work out."

Detective Burton went out the back sliding door.

"Leann," Detective Burton called back.

"Yes."

"Come over here and lock this door when I close it."

Leann went over to the door and locked it when Detective Burton closed it.

Detective Lee Burton walked the perimeter of the house.

Then he thought, *just what you need in a safe house. Flat landscaping. No large shrubbery to hide behind.*

Detective Burton checked around the outside of the house for about ten minutes. Then he went to the sliding door and knocked for Leann to let him back in the house.

It was then that he realized Leann probably heard him thinking.

Leann came to the back door and unlocked it to let Detective Burton back in the house.

"Thanks. It was getting pretty hot out there," Detective Burton stated, as he stepped inside the house and said, "I know it's only eleven fifteen Leann, but I am getting kind of hungry."

"Okay me too," Leann replied. "Would a sandwich be okay?"

"Yeah that is okay with me," Detective Burton said. "If anybody else wants anything different, they can fix that."

"What do you want to eat Meaghan?" Leann asked her.

"A sandwich is fine for me."

"Yeah," Detective Ryan said. "A sandwich is good."

"Okay then," Leann said. "We are having sandwiches."

Later that night at nine o'clock.

Detective Ryan had already went to his room.

Earlier that evening Detective Burton had explained to him that he wanted to catch anyone who tried to break in the house in a crossfire. So he put Detective Ryan in a bedroom on the opposite side of the house.

Detective Burton took the mattress out of the other extra bedroom and put it on the floor in Leann's and Meaghan's bedroom. He wanted to keep the three of them together.

"I sure am tired Leann," Meaghan said through a yawn.

"Hey Meaghan," Detective Burton said. "If you want to go to bed early, I'll sit out in the living room for a while. But Leann will stay in here with you. One of us has to stay with you at all times."

"Okay I am going to get a shower then," Meaghan said.

Then she gathered up her things and went into the bathroom.

"Okay Leann I have to tell you something that is just for you and me only. I don't want you to tell Meaghan or Ryan."

"Okay what is it?"

"I can't take the chance of anyone else hearing me. So I am going to sit in the living room and think what I want you to know. That way nobody will overhear me. I told you this would come in handy."

"Okay Lee. Go."

Detective Burton went to the kitchen and got a Diet Coke. Then he sat down on the couch.

"Okay Leann, I'm ready. Inside that trunk at the foot of the bed are two M-16s and six bandoliers of ammo. If something goes bad get to them. The trunk is steel plated with air holes at the bottom of the back. Put Meaghan in there. Nothing will shoot through that. If any-thing happens to me, I have a burner phone in my left front pocket. It will set off the four Claymore mines that I set up outside. Instead of wiring them up to the clackers, I wired them up to burner phones. The numbers are pre-set. As you are in the house looking at the front of the house, number one is the left side of the house. Number two is for the right side of the house. When you are looking at the back door looking out, number three is for the left side and of course number four is for

the right. Remember just you and me know this. Oh one more thing Leann, if you are wondering what a Claymore mine is just knock three times on the bedroom door."

Knock.

Knock.

Knock.

Detective Burton chuckled.

"Okay Claymore mines are used by the military. Each one is packed with C-4 and about seven hundred ball bearings. When they are set off they blow three hundred feet to the front and one hundred feet to the back of themselves. I have them set directly against the concrete slab of the house in front of a steel plate. So I am thinking the ones blown to the back will probably be thrust to the front as well. Okay I am done now."

In Detective Burton's master bedroom.

"Oh that feels so good," Meaghan said.

"I can imagine," Leann replied. "I am going to get a good hot shower now."

"Okay. I'll just brush my hair while you get your shower."

"If you want to wait until I get my shower, I'll brush your hair for you."

"Oh great. Then I can brush your hair for you."

"All right, you've got a deal," Leann said smiling.

ONE WEEK LATER

Chapter 16

Leanne said, with a yawn, "It's eleven o'clock guys. I am going to turn in. Excuse me."

"Yeah, I think I'll go to bed too," Meaghan said. "All that swimming today really made me tired."

"Okay you two," Detective Burton said. "Sleep well. I'll sneak in later. I won't wake you up. I promise."

Detective Ryan went to his room about ten o'clock.

Detective Burton was the only one left in the living room.

At one o'clock a.m. Detective Burton was still awake. He was reading the paper and working crossword puzzles. He had the paper delivered to the safe house so everybody could read it to help pass the time.

At one twenty a.m. Detective Burton thought he heard the faint sound of a car door shutting.

He ran to the garage and stood on a milk crate so he could see out the garage door window. It was the only place he could look out without being seen. He saw the car very plain from the street light on the corner across the street.

He saw four men get out of the car dressed in black.

They were carrying automatic rifles of some kind.

Detective Burton ran back into the house. He left the living room lights on. To turn the lights off would alert the intruders they had been spotted. Besides with the lights on, he would be able to see them better when they came into the house.

He ran to Leann's and Meaghan's bedroom.

He locked the door behind him. They had the night-light on, just as he had told them to do. He could see pretty good by just the night-light.

"Leann," Detective Burton whispered as loud as he could. "Leann," he said again. "Get Meaghan up."

"What is it Lee?" Leann said half asleep. "I thought you were going to come in quietly without waking us up."

"There are four armed men outside. They all have automatic rifles. They parked a little way down from the house so they could come up the side of the house.

"Okay what do we do Lee?" Leann asked.

"Meaghan. Get in the trunk," Detective Burton told her firmly. "It is steel plated. You'll be safe in there. Don't come out until one of us comes to get you. I have to get something out first. It will make more room for you."

Detective Burton opened the trunk and took the two M-16s and the bandoliers of ammo out.

"Here put this vest on Leann. I got one for me too."

"Get in," Detective Burton said to Meaghan.

Meaghan got into the trunk and Detective Burton closed the lid.

"Here Leann. Take these," Detective Burton said, handing her an M-16 and three bandoliers.

"They must be planning on coming in the back door."

Detective Burton put his three bandoliers over his shoulder and neck.

Leann did the same.

"Have you ever fired an M-16 before Leann?" Detective Burton asked.

"Yes. We have all this stuff where I am from too."

"Good. Stay here with Meaghan. I'm going out to the living room to greet our guests."

"Okay."

"Lock the door behind me. It ain't much but it's better than nothing."

Detective Burton opened the door and went out to the living room and ducked behind the couch.

He heard the sliding glass door slide open.

Leann if you can hear me, remember you heard me say, this is the police. Drop your guns, before all of the gunfire started. I don't want you to have to lie.

Detective Burton heard the door slide shut.

I guess all four of them must be in. I heard the door slide shut.

Detective Burton raised up to see all four men standing in the living room.

He shot the farthest one three times. Two in the chest and one in the head.

The other three opened fire on him. He ducked down as they laid cover fire, so they could escape through the back door.

Detective Burton raised up again when the firing stopped.

Detective Ryan came running out of his room.

"What the hell!" He shouted.

"Cover that back door," Detective Burton told him.

Then he ran to the bedroom door where Leann and Meaghan were. He knocked three times on the door.

"Leann it's me, Lee. Get Meaghan and come out here quick. Put the other vest on her."

When Detective Burton turned around, one of the men was at the back door. He raised his M-16 with one arm.

Bang!!

Bang!!

Bang!!

The man at the back door went down.

The bedroom door opened.

Leann looked out.

"Does Meaghan have her vest on?" Detective Burton asked Leann.

"Yes. She has it on."

"Come on then. I'll cover the back door. Get in the car girls. You too Ryan."

So Leann, Meaghan and Detective Ryan ran out to the garage.

Detective Burton was right on their heels.

They all jumped into the Charger.

Detective Burton opened the garage door and pulled the Charger outside.

Two men came running into view.

Detective Burton turned the headlights on.

Thirty six rounds peppered the Charger's windshield.

Leann screamed.

Meaghan screamed.

Detective Ryan said, "What the hell?"

Detective Burton looked over at him and smiled.

"Bulletproof glass."

Then Detective Burton floored the Charger, running into one of the mob guys. He slammed into the hood, up the windshield, over the top of the car and down the trunk.

Detective Burton slammed on the brakes and made a sharp left turn, leaving the Charger sideways at the bottom of the driveway. He pulled his service weapon from its holster, rolled down the window and shot six times at the man left in the driveway.

As he was falling to the ground he pulled the trigger of his automatic rifle and sent a spray of bullets at the Charger. Two of the stray bullets went through the open window of the Charger, striking Detective Burton. One of them hit him in the chest and the other one in the right arm.

"Oh shit!" Detective Burton yelled out.

"What is it Lee," Leann asked.

"Don't worry Leann. Two of those wild shots hit me. One got me in the right arm."

"We have to get you to a hospital!" Leann shouted.

"No. Our priority is protecting Meaghan."

"But Lee your hurt!" Meaghan yelled. "You've been shot! You have to go to the hospital!"

"Calm down girls," Detective Burton replied. "I'll be okay. Hell, I've cut myself worse than this shaving."

"Lee are you sure?" Leann asked.

"Please girls. Go back into the house. It'll be all right. We should be safe here for the rest of the night. I don't think anyone else will be coming. If they do they are in for one hell of a surprise. 'Cause they've pissed me off now."

They were all still standing in the driveway.

Detective Burton was holding his service weapon down by his side. Blood was running down his arm.

"Girls go inside please. I'll be right in."

"Okay, come on Meaghan," Leann told her.

Leann and Meaghan went inside the house and closed the door.

Chapter 17

Detective Burton walked over to the man he had hit with the Charger and knocked to the edge of the grass.

He felt of his neck with his left hand.

"Dammit," Detective Burton said. "This guy is still alive."

Then Detective Burton heard the beautiful angel's voice, once again, run through his mind.

You must protect her at all cost Lee.

Detective Burton raised his gun and pointed it at the mob guy's head.

Bang!!

"Why don't you pull the car in the garage Ryan? And pull those two dead guys inside too."

"Okay Detective Burton."

"And those five or six houses where the lights came on when the shooting started."

"Yeah."

"Knock on those doors. Show them your badge. Tell them some kids set off some firecrackers and that we have everything under control."

"Okay. I got ya."

Detective Burton walked into the house.

"Lee, are you okay," Leann asked. "We heard another shot."

Then Detective Burton looked at Meaghan, who had a concerned look on her face.

"The guy I ran over was still alive. He's not anymore."

Leann and Meaghan looked at each other.

"Leann I'm going to need your help."

"Sure Lee what do you need?"

"I'm going to need you to take the bullet out of my arm."

"Okay come in the bathroom."

Then Detective Burton told Leann, "the other day when I was snooping around the house, I saw a first aid kit under the sink. It has alcohol wipes, gauze, tape and an elastic bandage in it."

"Okay," Leann replied, as she looked under the sink. "Got it."

"Open it up and get the tweezers out."

"Okay."

"Get the alcohol wipes, gauze squares, tape and the elastic bandage out."

Leann did as she was told.

"Okay Lee. I got it all."

"Help me out of this vest and get my shirt off."

Leann pulled the heavy Kevlar vest off. She threw it on the bathroom floor. She started unbuttoning Detective Burton's shirt. "Meaghan. Are you okay with helping me take care of Lee?"

"Yeah. Blood doesn't bother me."

"Take this side of his shirt," Leann told Meaghan.

"Okay I got it."

"Take his T-shirt off too."

Leann and Meaghan had Detective Burton undressed from the waist up.

"Now what?" Leann asked.

"Get the tweezers."

"Okay, I got them."

"Now put some water in the sink. I don't care if it's cold."

Leann filled the sink half full of water.

"Get a washcloth."

"Here," Meaghan said. "Use this one."

"I need you to wash my arm off from the shoulder down to the elbow."

"Here Leann," Meaghan said. "Let me do that."

She dipped the washcloth into the water and squeezed it out softly. She wiped the blood from Detective Burton's arm.

"Okay Meaghan. Hold the washcloth on the wound," Detective Burton stated.

"Okay I got it."

"Leann I want you to spread the tweezers apart the size of the hole. Then jam it in. That way you should be around the slug."

"Okay," Leann said.

Then Detective Burton said to Meaghan, "Okay take the washcloth off."

She took the washcloth off slowly.

"Now Leann spread the tweezers, and get ready to jam them into the bullet hole."

"Okay."

"Meaghan give that spot at the wound one more swipe."

Meaghan wiped over the wound again.

"Now Leann."

Leann jammed the tweezers into the bullet hole.

"Aaaaahhhhh!"

"I'm sorry Lee."

"Don't worry about it Leann. It's going to hurt. Squeeze the tweezers with both hands as hard as you can."

"Okay I got it."

"Pull it up fast and hard."

Leann did as she was told.

"Ooouuuwwww!"

"Washcloth Meaghan," Detective Burton said calmly.

"Oh okay," Meaghan replied, pushing the washcloth over the wound.

"Okay girls. We're almost there."

"Good," Meaghan sighed.

"Okay Leann. Get five or six of those gauze squares.

"Okay."

"Cut three strips of that white tape about six inches long."

Leann cut the three strips of tape.

"Meaghan."

"Yes Lee."

"Rub over the wound really good with the washcloth then dry it. Then Leann take those three strips of tape and pull the hole together as tight as you can. Then squeeze some of those alcohol wipes over the wound."

Leann opened four of the alcohol wipes and squeezed them onto the wound.

"Now get four gauze squares and put them over the wound and tape them on."

Leann did everything Detective Burton told her to do.

"Now take the elastic bandage and wrap it around my arm to hold it all on."

"I'll do it Leann."

Meaghan started to wrap the elastic bandage around Detective Burton's arm.

"Just wrap it firm Meaghan. It doesn't have to be too tight."

"Okay."

Meaghan finished wrapping Detective Burton's arm and put the fasteners in place.

"That is really good girls. That will be good until tomorrow when I can go to my doctor and get it cleaned out better and stitched up."

"I feel so much better knowing you are going to the doctor tomorrow," Leann said.

"Yeah me too," Meaghan replied.

"Leann will you hand me a couple of those Tylenol tablets…….maybe three."

Leann handed Detective Burton three Tylenol tablets.

"It is the garage door Lee," Leann whispered, as she picked up her M-16.

"Hold on Leann. It might be Ryan. I sent him around to some of the neighbors with a cover story."

"Oh okay. You mean a lie?" Leann asked

"Well, a cover story is not exactly a lie....... Yes a lie."

"Okay then," Leann said, through a big grin.

"Keep the rifle, just in case."

"Yeah."

Detective Burton had left the bedroom door open from when he had come in from outside.

He drew his service weapon. All three of them stared at the door coming in from the garage. The door opened and Detective Ryan stepped out from behind it.

All three of them breathed a sigh of relief.

"Hey it's just me!" Detective Ryan yelled.

Then Detective Burton said to Leann, "You had your chance Leann. You blew it."

"What?" Leann asked.

"Hey Ryan," Detective Burton said. "Go to your room. We are all going to try to get a few hours sleep. Then we'll leave in the morning. Obviously we have to find a new safe house."

"All right that sounds good to me."

"Hey Ryan."

"What?"

"Lock that door."

"Okay sorry."

"And the sliding glass door."

Detective Ryan went over to the sliding glass door and locked it."

"Okay girls. Back in the room. Leann would you lock the door please?"

"Sure I have got it Lee."

"Thanks."

"Okay Lee do you want to take the bed?" Leann asked.

"No you girls keep it. What I've got is the same thing, only lower."

"Okay then. Good night Lee," Leann said softly.

"Yeah, I hope you can sleep," Meaghan said sympathetically.

"Thanks girls, for offering me the bed."

"You're welcome," Leann replied.

Detective Burton turned off the light and got down on the floor, so he could roll into bed.

"Ouch."

"Are you okay Lee," came Leann's voice through the darkness.

"Yeah, I'm fine.

THE NEXT DAY

Chapter 18

In Captain Angelo's office.

"I've been expecting you guys. Come on in," the captain greeted them. "Is everybody okay?"

"Yeah, I guess we are," Detective Burton answered.

"What about you Detective Ryan?" Captain Angelo asked.

"Yeah I'm fine sir," Detective Ryan replied.

"Ladies?"

"Yes sir. We are okay," Leann responded.

"The main thing is that Meaghan is okay," Detective Burton spoke up. "That is our whole goal."

Then Captain Angelo said, "I found out early this morning that during the early-morning shoot out that you, Detective Burton, took a bullet in the chest and one in the arm."

"How in the …….Oh Leann."

"I had to report it Lee. He's my boss."

"Don't worry. I'm not blaming you Leann," Detective Burton said softly.

Then Captain Angelo said, "I am assuming you had your vest on, since there is no slug in your chest."

"That's right sir. I've had enough slugs in my chest to last me a lifetime."

"Look Lee, all I am trying to establish here is, are you still fit for active duty?"

"Yes sir. It's just a little minor inconvenience. I'm good to go. Ask Leann, she patched me up. It's nothing serious."

"He is right captain. It's nothing that will keep him from doing his job."

"Okay," the captain gave in.

"I'm sorry sir," Detective Burton apologized. "I just get upset when somebody tries to take me off of my job. I am assigned to protect Meaghan and that is what I am going to do."

"He's right sir," Meaghan spoke up. "He protected me from the attack on the safe house last night. I don't want anybody else but Detective Burton and Leann with me. I feel safe with them."

"Well I guess it's settled then," the captain said. "You can't get a much better review than that."

"Hey guys I just had a thought, and it left me," Detective Burton said. "Give me about thirty seconds of quiet so I can think."

"Okay," Captain Angelo replied. "Everyone quiet."

"Leann, tell the captain you need to see him in private. Then tell him to come out and tell Ryan to get a motel room for a couple of days, until we get a new safe house ready. That's it I'm done.

"Well I guess I lost it. I guess it wasn't that important anyway. But if I do think of it, I will let you all know."

"Okay, you do that," the captain replied.

"Oh captain, I have to see you in private for a minute," Leann said causally.

"I hope it's not about me."

"It's not about you Lee."

Detective Burton gave Detective Ryan a funny look as Leann and the captain went out of his office.

"Captain you have to tell Detective Ryan to get a motel room for a couple of days, so we can get a new safe house ready."

"Okay Leann. I know Detective Burton likes to get them set up and prepared for the worst. When Detective Ryan leaves I'll give Detective Burton the address to the new safe house so he can fix it up the way he wants it."

"Thanks captain."

Leann and Captain Gabriel Angelo came walking back into his office.

"Okay," the captain said. "We will have to find a new safe house and get it all fixed up for you. It will have to be supplied with food, towels and linens. So give me a couple of days. Detective Ryan you might as well get a motel room for a couple of days and relax. I'll find a place for Detective Burton, Leann and Meaghan until the house is ready. Meaghan made it clear that she wants to stay with them. Nothing against you Detective Ryan," the captain commented. "But I do have to do as Meaghan wishes.

"I understand," Detective Ryan replied. "I'll try to get a room at that same motel I was at before."

"That sounds good," the captain responded.

Chapter 19

In Detective Lee Burton's apartment.

"If you girls are rested enough, how would you like to take a ride with me?" Detective Burton asked Leann and Meaghan.

"Yeah that would be awesome," Meaghan replied enthusiastically.

"Sure Lee, if you think it is safe," Leann said, looking Detective Burton in the eyes.

"I would never put Meaghan at risk, or you either. Besides Ryan doesn't know where I live."

"Why would you say that?" Leann asked with a puzzled look on her face.

"Yeah. Why would you say that?" Meaghan echoed.

"Okay I'll tell you what I think. We got the first safe house in Captain Angelo's office."

"Yeah, right," Leann affirmed.

"There was me, you, Meaghan, Ryan and the captain in the office at the time."

"Right."

"I didn't tell anybody about the safe house. I'm sure you or Meaghan didn't mention it to anybody. And we both know the captain is okay, don't we Leann? That leaves Ryan. I think he's dirty."

"When did you figure out about the captain Lee?" Leann asked.

"We'll talk about that later. Right now we have to be extra careful of Ryan."

Then Meaghan said, "I think you are right Lee. I never did like that asshole."

"Language young lady," Detective Burton replied.

"Sorry."

"You don't hear Leann talk like that do you?"

"No. I never have. I said I was sorry."

"Okay. Don't worry about it," Detective Burton said, while massaging his right arm just below the gunshot wound.

Leann noticed and said, "are you okay Lee?"

"Yeah I'm good. Don't worry girls. As long as I'm alive, I won't let anything happen to you."

"We know," Meaghan said. "You already proved that."

"Okay," Detective Burton went on. "Getting back to what I was talking about."

"Oh yeah," Meaghan said. "Go ahead."

"I think it was Ryan who tipped the mob off to our location."

"I think you are right Lee," Leann agreed.

"I do too, as I said before," Meaghan replied.

"So we all need to be especially alert," Detective Burton informed Leann and Meaghan. "Not only do we have an enemy coming after us, but we also have an enemy among us. We have to make sure that when the shooting starts, we don't get shot in the back. And Leann, we have to keep Meaghan out of Ryan's reach at all times. The mob has a far reach, but nobody is that damn good."

"Why don't you guys just keep Ryan off your team?" Meaghan asked.

"It's not that easy Meaghan. We don't have any proof that it is him for sure. We have to catch him in the act, and if I do, I'll deal with him right on the spot."

"Okay I see," Meaghan replied.

"Hey you guys, what about that ride?"

"Yeah where are we going?" Meaghan asked.

"I need to prepare the new safe house for us. I have a feeling they're going to hit us a lot harder the second time."

"The second time," Meaghan said. "If you know they are coming back, why would you wait in the safe house for them?"

"Because that is the only way we can catch them. We don't know where they are. But after this we will. It's the only way to draw them out."

"But how will you know it is Ryan who tipped them off.?"

"Because hopefully they will have a phone record on their cell phones. The last guys had deleted all of their phone records and destroyed the SIM cards before they hit us. These guys most likely text each other. In that case we can get a good SIM card and plug it into a SIM card reader and we can retrieve all of the deleted text messages. We'll just have to wait and see. Besides Ryan is the only one of us who would tell the mob."

"Okay Lee, we trust you," Leann injected into the conversation.

"I'm counting on Ryan's phone if he is dirty. Don't worry Meaghan," Detective Burton told her. "I would never put you in any danger. I have a plan."

"I'm not worried Lee," Meaghan replied.

"You can count on Lee, Meaghan."

"I know Leann."

"Okay ladies, the ride," Detective Burton said. "I have to make a call. Then we are going to see a friend of mine."

Chapter 20

Detective Lee Burton called his friend at the body shop.

"Hi Grayson. It's Detective Burton. Can I rent one of your pickups today?"

"Sure when do you need it?"

"In about an hour."

"Okay I got one left. My guys are out picking up parts in the others. I'll hold the truck for you Lee."

"Thanks Grayson. I'll see you in an hour or so."

"Okay."

"Don't worry Grayson. I'll fill it up with gas before I bring it back."

"I'm not worried Lee."

"Hey Grayson."

"Yeah."

"I'm going to be bringing two pretty women with me and I'm going to have a Charger parked on your lot until we get back."

"Sure that's fine. I'll watch it for you."

"Thanks buddy. Bye."

"Bye Lee."

"Okay girls, let's go."

Chapter 21

In forty three minutes Detective Burton, Leann and Meaghan pulled into the parking lot of Grayson's Body Shop and parked under a sign that read FREE BREAK INSPECTIONS.

Grayson came walking out of one of the work bays.

"Hi Lee. It's good to see you."

"Yeah it's good to see you too Grayson. How's business?"

"It's good Lee. Really good."

Then Detective Burton turned to Leann and Meaghan and said, "These two beautiful ladies are Leann here and her friend Meaghan."

"Hi ladies," Grayson said smiling. "It is a pleasure to meet you both."

"They are going to be helping me at the house."

"Oh, you bought a house?"

"No. It's somebody ease's house. They are going to help me get it ready. Is that the truck?"

"Yeah that's it."

"I hate to ask for the moon here. But could we borrow your two wheeler again?"

"It's already strapped in the bed, along with the other stuff you wanted."

"Thanks Grayson. I hate to run, but I don't have a lot of time to get the house ready."

"I understand."

"See you later Grayson. Let's go ladies I'll show you how to get a house ready for our guests. This party should be a real blast."

Detective Burton and the girls got in the pickup and headed for the safe house.

On the way out of the parking lot Leann said to Detective Burton, "I have noticed how you do not really lie to people, you just do funny things to the truth."

Chapter 22

Thirty five minutes later Detective Lee Burton pulled off Highway 101 and took the back-roads to the safe house.

From the street Detective Burton punched the garage door opener and backed the truck half way into the garage.

They all got out of the truck and looked around.

"Would you girls get that two wheeler for me please? I'm trying not to hurt my arm any more that I have to."

"Don't worry about it Leann," Meaghan said. "I'll get it. I used to help my dad do stuff all the time."

"Thanks Meaghan," Leann said with a big smile.

Meaghan untied the two wheeler, slid it down the tailgate and took it into the house.

"Right over there is good hon," Detective Burton said. "Thank you."

"You're welcome Lee."

"I am going to see if there is still any bottled water in the refrigerator. Sorry but I need to take a little break. Just give me five minutes."

"Sit down on the couch Lee," Meaghan told him. "I'll get the water for you."

"Thank you."

Detective Burton walked into the living room and sat down on the couch.

Meaghan brought a bottle of water for him, Leann and herself.

"Thank you Meaghan," Detective Burton said. "You're a good kid."

"Thanks Lee."

"I don't want you girls to worry because I'm resting. When the trouble comes, and it will come, I'll be ready. I won't let the arm stand in my way."

"We are not worried that you cannot do your job Lee," Leann replied. "We are just concerned about you."

"Thanks girls. I appreciate it."

Detective Burton finished the last of his bottle of water.

"We had better get that trunk loaded girls. That will be the worst thing we have to do. With all of that steel plating it is pretty heavy. I hope you girls didn't mind coming along with me."

"No, we do not mind at all Lee," Leann told him.

Then Meaghan said, "Of course not. We would have just been sitting around anyway. It's good to get out."

"The truth is I thought I might need your help loading that damned heavy trunk."

"It is okay Lee," Leann answered him.

Detective Burton grabbed the two wheeler and walked into the bedroom.

"Okay girls if you can just pick the front of the trunk up about a quarter of an inch, that is all I need. And keep your fingers on the ends of the trunk."

"Okay Meaghan lift," Leann told her. "We will get it."

The girls strained to lift the heavy trunk.

As soon as Detective Burton saw the trunk raise he shoved the blade of the two wheeler under it.

"Good job girls. Now all we have to do is get it into the bed of the truck. And I have an idea."

Detective Burton pushed the trunk out to the door going into the garage.

"Okay girls, get in the garage. I am going to have to bump it through the doorway and let it fall onto the garage floor. Get your hands on it to help steady the thing."

"Okay we got it Lee," Leann said.

Detective Burton bumped the trunk through the doorway and the two wheeler's wheels fell onto the garage floor.

Leann and Meaghan immediately put their hands on the trunk. It started tipping forward and they pushed as hard as they could until the trunk fell back onto the two wheeler.

"Good girls. Good."

"Whew," Leann said. "You were not lying about that trunk being heavy."

"You know me Leann. I never lie. I just do funny things with the truth."

Leann and Meaghan laughed.

Detective Burton smiled, really big.

"Okay," Detective Burton said. "You girls see how that driveway goes down right before the street?"

"Yes," they both said, at the same time.

"I'm going to drive the truck down there. Then when I get the back tires in the dip the tailgate should only be about a foot from the ground."

"Okay I see," Leann replied. "I get it."

"It will be a whole lot easier than trying to lift that monster up four feet. I'm going to turn the two wheeler around and bump it against the wall so it doesn't move. All I need you girls to do is just balance it until I get back."

"Okay," Leann said.

"Sure we got it," Meaghan responded.

"Okay there it is. Don't let it slip away girls."

"We won't," they said simultaneously.

Detective Burton got in the truck and drove it down to the dip in the driveway. He got out of the truck to check its position. Then he got back in and pulled the truck up a couple of feet more.

Then he got out of the truck and looked at it again.

"Good enough."

Detective Burton went back to the garage and got the two wheeler.

"Okay I'm going to push this down to the truck. Then I'm going to need you girls to help me push it into the truck bed. C'mon."

"Okay," Leann said.

"Okay," Meaghan replied.

Leann and Meaghan followed Detective Burton down the driveway to the back of the truck.

"All right girls. This won't be too bad. We're going to use leverage."

"Okay Lee," Leann said. "Just tell us what you want us to do."

"Help me turn the trunk up on its end, the tall way. Just stand it up on the two wheeler. Let's all get on a side. You girls each take a side of that end and I'll hold this end with my left arm, so it doesn't slide. Ready?"

"Yeah we are ready." Leann said.

"Lift."

Everybody grunted and groaned.

They lifted the trunk up on its end.

"All right that was good," Detective Burton said. "As he let out a big breath.

"Now what?" Meaghan asked.

"Let's push it until the bottom leans against the tailgate."

They all pushed the trunk until it fell against the tailgate.

"Okay girls. Let's all pick this end up until it is level and then shove it into the truck bed. Okay now."

They all grabbed the trunk and lifted it up until it was level, then they pushed it into the back of the truck.

"Great," Detective Burton said. "I think you deserve to go out and eat when we get the new safe house set up."

"That sounds good to me," Leann said.

"Yeah me too," Meaghan replied cheerfully. "Can I pick the place?"

"You sure can hon," Detective Burton answered. "Meaghan would you mind tying the trunk in place, while I untie the cardboard box and get the Claymores and the Turf Builder."

"Sure."

"Leann."

"Yes Lee."

"Would you please follow me and get the Turf Builder and the Claymores and put them in the truck for me. They're not heavy."

"Yeah. I will get them for you."

When Leann and Detective Burton were done collecting the Claymore mines and the Turf Builder, Detective Burton secured them in the cardboard box in the back of the truck.

"Thanks girls. Unloading will be much easier. I promise."

"I sure hope so," Leann said.

"I'll be right back girls. Wait here."

Detective Burton went through the safe house. He made sure it was all secured.

Then he went back out to the pickup.

"Let's go girls."

They all got into the pickup.

Detective Burton put on his seat belt and said, "the house is going to need some serious remodeling after all of those bullet holes."

"Yes, it is a shame," Leann commented. "It is such a nice house."

"It sure is," Meaghan agreed.

Detective Burton, Leann and Meaghan drove off to the new safe house.

Chapter 23

In forty seven minutes Detective Burton, Leann and Meaghan drove up in front of the new safe house.

"Let me open it," Meaghan said.

"Okay, I think you've earned it," Detective Burton told her, handing her the garage door opener.

Meaghan pushed the button and watched the garage door roll up into the garage.

"Okay Lee," Meaghan stated. "Back this bad boy in there so we can get done. I'm getting hungry."

"Yeah, you and me both."

"Yeah you two, and me too," Leann said, and then started laughing.

Leann was a beautiful woman with a contagious laugh.

So Detective Burton and Meaghan started laughing too.

Once all of the laughing was done.

Detective Burton pulled the truck up and backed up the driveway and half way into the garage.

When he turned around he saw a man walking up the driveway.

"Sit still girls," Detective Burton told them.

He reached to his hip and pulled his service weapon out of its holster and held it against the door.

Detective Burton scanned the area for other men or movement.

He rolled down his driver's side window and said to the man,

"Hello sir. How are you doing?"

"I'm fine. How are you folks?"

"We're good. It sure is nice today isn't it?"

"Yes," the man replied. "It is. Are you folks moving in?"

"No," Detective Burton answered. "We are just going to be here for a couple of weeks, maybe less. It's just a little family getaway."

The more Detective Burton talked to the man the less of a threat he considered him to be.

"Oh by the way, my name is Paul. The wife and me live right there across the street."

"All right," Detective Burton said, putting his gun in his left hand and stretching his right hand out the window to shake Paul's hand. "Take it easy on the shake Paul. I hurt my arm a few days ago."

"Okay," Paul answered, shaking Detective Burton's hand gently.

"My name is Lee. That's my wife Leann and our daughter Meaghan."

"Nice to meet you all."

"Yeah you too," Leann replied.

Then Paul said, "I take it it's just the three of you."

"That's right," Detective Burton answered. "But we are expecting some company while we're here. I'm not exactly sure when they are coming. But things could get loud. They're a bunch of party animals. So I must apologize in advance if it gets noisy."

"I'm sure it will be fine," Paul replied.

"I hate to rush you off Paul. But we have to get this stuff unloaded. Leann and Meaghan want to go out to eat when we're done here. I did promise them."

"Oh sure. I know how it is," Paul said, as he turned away and walked down the driveway.

"All right then," Detective Burton blurted out. "We'll see you around."

"Sure thing," Paul said, from half way down the driveway.

"Tell you wife hi for me!" Leann shouted.

"Will do!"

Detective Burton holstered his service weapon and said to Leann, "I wanted to ask him so bad to help us unload that trunk. But if he had noticed it was steel plated, I think it would have raised too many questions."

"I think you are right Lee," Leann responded. "We might have had a little trouble explaining the M-16s and the body armor too."

"I'm sure."

"Okay let's get this stuff unloaded," Meaghan said. "So we can go eat, mom and dad."

Detective Burton and Leann couldn't help but laugh.

THE NEXT DAY

Chapter 24

At nine seventeen that morning Detective Burton along with Detective Robins, Detective Ryan and Meaghan pulled the dull red Dodge Charger into the driveway of the new safe house.

"Well here we are kids," Detective Burton announced. "Home sweet home."

"Yes you got that right," Leann agreed.

"I hope this house is better than the last one," Detective Burton spoke out.

"Yeah," Meaghan replied.

"I sure do too," Leann said.

Then Detective Burton said, "Actually the other house was fine. The problem was those assholes who tried to kill us. If anybody else comes I won't be so easy on 'em."

"Yeah you are right Lee," Leann said.

Detective Burton handed the garage door opener to Meaghan and said, "Hit it."

Meaghan hit the open button and Detective Burton drove the Charger into the garage.

"Okay everybody let's get settled in," Detective Burton told them.

Everybody got out of the car and got their suitcase out of the trunk.

Detective Burton handed the house keys to Meaghan.

"You want to open the door?"

"Sure."

Meaghan opened the door and took her suitcase into the master bedroom.

Leann followed her with her suitcase.

Detective Ryan walked in with his suitcase and sat it down in the living room.

Detective Burton came in and said, "I'm sure there is an extra bedroom down there someplace."

"I'll find it."

Then Detective Burton took his suitcase into the master bedroom and joined Leann and Meaghan.

"Does somebody want to help me drag the extra bedroom mattress in here?"

"Sure let me help you Lee," Leann replied."

Later that evening.

"That sure was a great meal Meaghan," Detective Burton commented. "You will make some lucky young man a good wife, being able to cook like that."

"Yes that was excellent," Leann replied.

"It definitely was good," Detective Ryan agreed.

"I noticed a cherry pie in the fridge, if anyone wants dessert," Meaghan said.

"Not me," Detective Burton said. "I'm stuffed. But maybe later."

"Yes I will have some later too," Leann replied. "That sounds good."

"I'll take mine right now," Detective Ryan said.

"I will get it Meaghan," Leann told her, in an effort to keep Meaghan as far away from Detective Ryan as possible.

Leann went to the refrigerator and pulled out the cherry pie and cut a slice out. She put it on a plate and put it in the microwave for twenty two seconds and put it on the table in front of Detective Ryan.

"Thank you Leann."

"You're welcome."

Everybody moved into the living room while Detective Ryan ate his piece of pie.

Later that night at eight o'clock.

"Okay girls," Detective Burton said. "Let's go get set up in the bedroom so we're not taken by surprise."

"Okay," Leann replied. "Come on Meaghan come with me."

"Okay."

"Once again Ryan," Detective Burton said to him. "If you are in one of the extra bedrooms we can get them in a crossfire."

"Got ya."

Detective Burton watched Detective Ryan go into the bedroom on the right side of the hallway.

Then he went into the master bedroom with Leann and Meaghan.

"All right girls. Listen up," Detective Burton said, as he walked over to the trunk and opened the lid.

"I have something new to show you."

Detective Burton reached inside the trunk and pulled out a box. He opened it up and took out a small monitor, closing the lid back down.

"Here Meaghan, plug this in."

"What is it?"

"It's a small monitor for the camera I put above the front door.

"Meaghan plugged the monitor into a wall plug by the night stand.

"See how you can see everything all the way out to the street?"

"Yeah this is really so cool Lee," Meaghan said.

"It sure is," Leann said. "I wish we would have had this at the other house."

"So do I girls," Detective Burton said. "That's why I got this one now. I had Grayson pick it up for me. He's a good kid."

"Yeah he sure seems like it," Leann agreed.

Detective Burton walked over to the trunk and opened the lid.

"Leann get an M-16 and three bandoliers of ammo and a vest out of here. Get Meaghan's vest too. Put them somewhere where you can get to them easily. I'm going to put mine over there by the door."

"Okay Lee. I will take care of it."

"I'm going to take a quick shower and change clothes while you girls watch the monitor."

"Okay," they both said, getting really good at answering at the same time.

"Here's the burner phone Leann."

"Okay thanks."

"Everything is programmed in it already. If you see them coming before I get done, wait until they all get past the sidewalk. Then push buttons one and two. One right after the other. That will kill them even if they are wearing body armor. The shrapnel to the head will do the job. Trust me. We used them in the army."

"I got it Lee."

"Just make sure Meaghan is in the trunk, just in case."

"I will."

"I'll be right back girls."

"Yeah, okay," Leann said.

"I'll be really quick."

"Okay hurry," Leann said nervously.

Chapter 25

Detective Burton took a quick shower and put on fresh clothes. He was back in twelve minutes.

"Hey girls are we still okay?" Detective Burton asked, as he picked up the burner phone from the bed and put it in his pocket.

"Yes, we are still okay," Leann answered.

"Lee," Meaghan said.

"Yeah hon."

"Why are we all in this room and Detective Ryan in another room? Why didn't you tell him about the monitor and the Claymore mines?"

171

"That's nothing for you to worry about sweetie. But the reason is, as I told you before, because I suspect he is dirty. You know what that means don't you?"

"You think he's a bad cop."

"Yes that's exactly what I think. Because he gets the address to the safe house when we all get it as a group, and the mob found us in the first safe house. Plus I check the locks on the doors and windows every thirty minutes while I'm awake. You know that. In the first safe house I was waiting for them behind the couch. The mob guys just slid the door right open. Ryan had to slip out and unlock the door for them when I went to the bathroom."

"Really?"

"Yes, but this time it will be different. We have the monitor. We will see anybody as soon as they pull up. Leann and I will watch in shifts."

"What are you going to do with Detective Ryan?"

"As soon as this is all over, we are going to arrest him and take him in. If somebody finds us once, that could be a fluke. But twice, I don't think so. That's why we have to do this again. We have to be sure he's tipping them off."

"So if somebody comes after us again, you'll be sure?"

"That is right," Leann told Meaghan.

Then Detective Burton said, "the next safe house we go to I am going to pick. Just Leann and I and you will know where it is. Nobody will find us."

"Okay Lee. I trust you and Leann to protect me."

"I am so glad you do. That makes me feel good," Detective Burton replied.

Thirty minutes after that conversation.

"Lee," Leann whispered.

"What?"

"Three black SUVs just drove up in front of the house."

"Okay," Detective Burton said, as he put on his bullet-proof vest and picked up his M-16 and bandoliers of ammo.

"Leann watch that monitor very close. Meaghan get in the trunk. I'm going to watch them through the garage door window."

"I have the burner phone that controls the Claymores Leann."

"Okay."

"I don't want you to have to do that."

"Thanks Lee, I do not think that would go over very well."

Detective Burton ran out to the garage. He saw four men with automatic rifles get out of each SUV from the top of the milk crate he brought from the first safe house.

"Well love me," Detective Burton said.

Detective Burton watched intently as the men started walking toward the house. He watched until they were about five feet past the sidewalk. He pulled the burner phone from his left front pocket and pushed button number one. He heard the electronic beeps as the burner phone dialed the phone wired to the left Claymore mine. He knew it would take three seconds to complete the circuit.

BOOM!!!!!

The first Claymore mine went off throwing ball bearings three hundred feet forward with a tremendous force.

Then Detective Burton pushed button number two for the right Claymore.

Three seconds later.

BOOM!!!!!

Another blast thrust forth the deadly ball bearings.

Detective Burton scanned the front lawn.

Twelve men were lying on the lawn.

Detective Burton was scanning the front area of the lawn when he saw another black SUV pull up in front of the house.

Four men with automatic rifles got out.

"Holy dog snot," Detective Burton whispered. "These shit heads just don't quit."

They started heading around the side of the house to the back door.

Detective Burton ran back in the house and got behind the couch.

Leann ran out of the bedroom and got behind the recliner.

"Leann get back in the bedroom. You don't have any protection there."

"I have my vest on."

"That's not what I mean."

It was too late. Detective Burton saw the men at the back sliding glass door.

He could see them really good from the glow of the neighbors back porch light.

They slid the door open and walked into the house.

Detective Burton gave them enough time to get in the house, then he raised up and yelled, "Drop your guns boys!!" Knowing they would not drop their guns.

The men turned quickly toward Detective Burton and opened fire as he ducked behind the couch. The bullets peppered the couch to the sound of dings, pings and clangs.

After the bullets stopped coming, Detective Burton know they had to reload.

He raised up from behind the couch and fired in bursts of three rounds.

Bang! Bang! Bang!

Bang! Bang! Bang!

Bang! Bang! Bang!

Bang! Bang! Bang!

Detective Burton took down the four mobsters.

Leann raised up from behind the recliner and looked at Detective Burton.

Just then they heard footsteps coming down the hallway.

Detective Burton motioned for Leann to get behind the recliner as he ducked behind the couch.

The footsteps got closer.

"Detective Burton. Detective Robins. Are you guys okay? I think we got 'em all."

Leann don't move. Don't answer. Detective Burton thought really fast. *Stay behind the recliner. I'm looking at Ryan right now with my left eye. He has his gun raised and he don't look very friendly. I'm going to draw him away from you.*

Detective Burton raised up from behind the couch and walked to the other end away from Leann.

"Ryan, it is you. I would have got up sooner but I wasn't sure for a while that it was you. I still have the sound of gunfire ringing in my ears."

"Where's Detective Robins?"

"Well, she's supposed to be in the bedroom guarding Meaghan."

"Why don't you turn the light on Ryan?"

Detective Ryan walked over to the light switch with his gun still in his hand.

Detective Burton walked out from behind the couch, farther away from Leann, with his service weapon in his hand.

Detective Ryan flipped the light switch on.

"Wow. You sure took care of those guys Burton. You some kind of a military vet?"

"Yeah. United States Army Special Forces."

"Well, that explains how you took out all of these mob guys without breakin' a sweat."

"Yeah," Detective Burton said. "How do you think they keep finding us?"

"It's hard to say. They have a long reach."

"Yeah you're right Ryan. I'll bet they have people every-where."

Then Detective Burton saw Detective Ryan's eyes change. He knew what he was going to do next.

Detective Ryan raised his gun.

Detective Burton raised his gun.

Three shots rang out and echoed through the house.

Bang!!

Bang!!

Bang!!

Detective Ryan fell to the floor as he squeezed off a shot.

Detective Burton slowly looked over at the recliner.

"No!"

Leann was standing up behind it with her arms stretched out over the back. Little swirls of smoke were rolling up from the barrel of her service weapon.

Detective Burton holstered his gun and slowly walked over to Leann. Her grabbed her gun by the barrel and slowly pulled it from her hands.

"Are you okay Leann?"

"Yes. I am okay."

Detective Burton grabbed Leann by the arms and sat her down in the recliner.

"What's going to happen to you now Leann?" Detective Burton asked softly.

"I don't know Lee."

"Maybe nothing," Detective Burton said. "Look at me. I made it to heaven once. I'm sure God will forgive you."

"I hope so Lee."

Then Detective Burton said, with the saddest look on his face, "I wish I could make it back to heaven again. But now I'm not so sure Leann."

"Why? What do you mean?"

"Well, those twelve guys lying out there on the front lawn. Then those four right over there. Then there's the other four guys who attacked us the other day. That's twenty men I've killed just this week."

"But you were protecting Meaghan, as you were told to do."

"And you were protecting me." Detective Burton whispered.

"Yes," Leann whispered.

"I think you will be all right Leann."

"Yeah but tell me one thing Lee. That couch is riddled with bullets, and all that dinging noise. How are you still okay?

"I had Grayson come by the night before we got here. He screwed a steel plate to the back of the couch."

"Yes, I guess if you are going to protect Meaghan, you have to protect yourself too."

"My God Meaghan," Detective Burton said. "Let's get her out of the trunk."

"Okay."

Detective Burton and Leann went into the master bedroom and opened the trunk lid.

Meaghan screamed.

"It's okay sweetie. It is me and Lee."

Meaghan stood up quickly and hugged Leann.

"I was so scared. I thought with all of that shooting you and Lee were dead."

"No honey, we are okay," Leann replied.

"Lee."

"Yes. I'm good too."

"I'm so glad you are both okay."

"I have to call this in girls. Then how would you like to go to my apartment for the rest of the night?"

"I think that would be a good idea," Leann said.

"Yeah, me too."

"Okay girls, pack your things and put them in the Charger. I'm going to get Ryan's phone so we can check it out. Then I'll call this in. I'll have the team that comes out here get all of the other guy's phones. We have to wait at least until the other guys get here before we can leave. But I would like to get out of here before the neighbors start flocking over here."

"Yeah," Meaghan uttered. "If they're not too afraid to come over."

"I think that might be the case," Detective Burton affirmed.

Chapter 26

Leann, Detective Burton and Meaghan lugged their suitcases into his apartment living room.

"Just leave them setting right there girls. Are you hungry?"

"Yeah I'm hungry," Meaghan said.

"Yes, I am too," Leann answered.

"Well then, that makes three of us. I think we are pretty safe for the night. Would you like to go out and get something to eat? Or would you like to order in?"

"I'm still shaking like a leaf Lee," Meaghan answered. "Could we just have something delivered here?"

"Sure we can. You want to pick something?"

"Sure I'll look through the menus."

Meaghan went to the drawer where Detective Burton kept his menus.

Detective Burton said to Leann, "are you really okay Leann?"

"Yeah sure. I am okay Lee."

"Good as soon as Meaghan figures out something to eat, we'll order it, eat and then kick back for a while. I don't think I'll get much sleep tonight. I usually don't anyway."

"I know Lee."

"Hey you guys," Meaghan said. "Would you like to have a Philly Cheese steak Sandwich?"

"Oh yeah, that sounds great," Detective Burton answered. "We have plenty of chips to have with it."

"It comes with fries."

"Okay, that's cool too."

"Do they have any hamburgers?" Leann asked.

"No they don't."

"You'll like these too Leann. I'm sure," Detective Burton told her."

"They have sides you can get with them," Meaghan said.

"Get whatever you and Leann want with yours. I'm good with the fries."

"Can I interest you in some coleslaw Lee?"

"Yeah get me that. I'm going to run in and take a quick shower and change.......again."

"Okay," Leann replied.

"Here put the food on this credit card Meaghan."

"Thanks Lee."

Detective Burton took a long hot shower and changed his clothes.

He was back in twenty minutes.

Ten minutes later there was a knock on the door.

Detective Burton opened the door to see a pretty brunette holding three bags in her hands.

"Come on in young lady," Detective Burton said to her. "Just set the bags right there on the table."

"Okay. There you are sir. Have a good night."

"Wait a minute," Detective Burton said.

"Is there something wrong sir?" The young brunette asked.

"No. Just hang on a minute. Meaghan did you leave the tip on the card?"

"No. I thought you wanted to give it in cash."

"I do."

Detective Burton reached in his pocket and pulled out his paper money. He peeled off a twenty dollar bill and gave it to the young girl.

"Thank you sir. You all have a great night."

"You too," Leann replied.

"Oh this stuff smells so good," Detective Burton said.

"Yes it sure does," Leann agreed.

Detective Burton, Leann and Meaghan ate and talked for almost an hour.

"Well girls it's four o'clock. I'm going to lie down and rest for a while. Meaghan you can sleep with Leann again. I'll take the other bedroom."

"Great. That sounds good to me," Leann said.

"I don't think either one of us will sleep any more tonight. We might just lie around and have some girl talk," Leann told Detective Burton.

"That sounds good Leann," Meaghan said.

"Well I hate to run off to bed girls, but gunfights kind of tire me out."

"Yeah I am sure," Leann replied.

Chapter 27

The next morning in Captain Angelo's office.

"Good morning captain," Detective Burton greeted him.

"Good morning Detective Burton, Detective Robins, Meaghan," the captain replied. "How is everybody doing after that fiasco last night?"

"We are all good captain," Leann answered.

"I don't want to be rude captain," Detective Burton said. "But I need to get right to the point. I trust you and I know you're okay, and Leann knows why. Now I need a list of safe houses available. Just put the list on your desk and go for a cup of coffee. I'll pick one and write it down on a piece of paper. Leann and I will be the only ones who know where it is, and of course Meaghan. But as an extra precaution, I will set this house up the way I want it to be, and it won't take two days."

Captain Angelo opened his desk drawer and put the list of safe houses on his desk.

Then the captain said, "Good luck Lee," as he walked out of his office

Leann can you still hear me thinking?

Detective Burton looked over at Leann.

She gave him a big exaggerated smile.

Okay then. Let's take the third one down from the top, the one on Pecos Road. Would you write the address down for me please?

Leann picked up a piece of paper and a pen from the desk and wrote down the address to the safe house on Pecos Road.

"Good," Detective Burton said. "I'll take that. Thank you."

"You are welcome Lee."

"Okay Meaghan we're going."

"Where are we going now?" Meaghan asked.

"Right now we are all going out for a nice well deserved lunch," Detective Burton replied. "It's a little bit out of the way, but I would like to take you girls to Applebee's."

"Oh great!" Meaghan exclaimed. "We have Applebee's in Chicago too. I go to the one on Cicero Avenue all the time with my girlfriends."

"Do they have hamburgers there Lee?"

"Yes Leann. They have hamburgers there," Detective Burton said, smiling at Leann's obsession with hamburgers.

"Good. Let us go," Leann said enthusiastically.

"All right awesome," Meaghan responded.

"Hey girls. After we have lunch, would you like to go by Target and buy a deck of cards and some board games? That way we'll have something to do to pass the time."

"Sure," Meaghan replied. "That will be fun."

"I'll leave it up to you to pick them out," Detective Burton told Meaghan.

FOUR HOURS LATER

Chapter 28

In Detective Lee Burton's apartment.

"Okay, you girls should be perfectly safe here," Detective Burton said. "I'm going to go by Grayson's Body Shop and rent his pickup one last time."

"What are you going to do now?" Leann asked.

"I want to go by the other safe house and get the trunk, just to be safe. I don't think we will have any more trouble, but I'm not slackin' off. I already have the two Claymores and the Turf Builder from the back yard in the trunk. That should be all we'll need. On the way to get the pickup I'll stop by Target and get a new camera. I need to get them set up in the front yard of the new safe house. I really like the new house."

"Yeah, we do to," Meaghan said.

"I have to go girls."

"Okay Lee. Be careful," Leann urged.

"Yeah, watch yourself," Meaghan said.

"I will girls. I should be back in about five hours or so. Then I would like to spend the night here and hit the safe house in the morning after we go out for breakfast."

"Wow Lee, you are pulling out all the stops," Leann commented.

"Yeah," Meaghan responded. "What did we do to deserve this?"

"Well I'll tell ya girls. We have been through some rough times these last couple of weeks. I just want to do something nice for you."

"Thanks Lee," Leann said. "You are a good man."

"Leann is right Lee. If it wasn't for you and her, I would probably be dead right now."

Then Detective Burton said to Meaghan, "There are other good cops out there too Meaghan."

"I'm sure there is Lee, but I still want you and Leann looking after me."

"You don't have to worry about that hon," Detective Burton assured her. "That's the plan, and that came right from the top."

"Good. Because I like you and Leann."

"We like you too. You're a good girl."

"Yes, you sure are," Leann agreed. "You are doing the right thing."

"Thank you guys."

"Well girls, I had better get going so I can make it back in time for dinner. But if I am not back in time, don't wait for me. Just go ahead and eat."

"Are you sure you are not expecting trouble Lee?" Leann asked.

"Yes I am sure. I just meant if I get stuck in heavy traffic or if it takes me a little longer setting up the house than I had planned. Because it always takes longer than I plan."

"Okay Lee," Leann said. "You had better get going so you can get back in time to eat with us. Because we are going to wait for you. Right Meaghan?"

"Right."

"Okay then, I'll see you girls when I get back."

"Okay," Meaghan answered.

Chapter 29

Detective Lee Burton went by Grayson's Body Shop and rented his pickup and the two wheeler.

"Hey Grayson how's it goin'?"

"Good Lee. Real good."

"I promise I won't be bugging you for a while after this."

"Hey don't worry about it Lee. I'm making extra money from you."

"Do you have a soft drink machine that I could buy a bottle of water from?"

"I can do better than that Lee. I have a refrigerator in my office. I'll get you a bottle of water on me."

"Hey don't trouble yourself. Here's my credit card. You write up the truck and I'll get the water myself."

"Thanks Lee. I'll write this up for you so you can get going. I remember when you called you said you were taking the wife and daughter out to eat tonight. That way you can get your little project done and get home in time."

Detective Burton knew something was off. Grayson knew he wasn't married.

"Thanks Grayson. I can't keep the little woman waiting. You know how they get."

Detective Burton looked around the shop, like he should have when he first walked through the door. The sun shining through the open bay door was casting a shadow on the wall of a hand holding a gun.

Detective Burton went into Grayson's office and got the bottle of water. He needed to take some Ibuprofen for his arm. He also knew he had to get Grayson out of the line of fire.

"Hey Grayson I hate to keep bothering you, but could you run out and see if your guy is going to have my truck done by two o'clock tomorrow?"

"Sure Lee. I'll go ask him right now."

"Good, thanks."

As soon as Grayson was out of the line of fire Detective Burton spun around and dove into the boxes the robber was hiding behind.

He grabbed the man's gun hand on the way to the floor.

Detective Burton was using all of the strength he had in his right arm to keep the gun pointed away from his head. His right arm was throbbing. He banged the man's hand on the floor until the gun flew out of his hand and went sliding across the floor.

He picked the man up by the shirt and slammed his head against the wall.

The man broke free from Detective Burton's grip and punched him in the jaw. That sent him falling backward over the boxes on the floor.

The man ran for his gun. As he was bending down to pick up the gun, Detective Burton was drawing his service weapon from its holster.

The man turned and raised his gun and pointed it at Detective Burton.

Detective Lee Burton fired his gun once.

BANG!!

The bullet ripped through the man's chest.

Detective Burton knew the man was dead.

God help me. Detective Burton thought. *I'm sorry God. I know it was you who did help me. You gave me the burst of strength I needed to come out on top of the altercation. Thank you for that. And thank you for Leann too.*

"Lee are you okay?" Grayson asked.

"Yeah. Come on in."

"Lee. You've got blood running down your arm."

"Oh shit. Leann is really going to be upset. Oouuch."

"Hey Grayson will you do something for me please?"

"Anything Lee."

"I can't stick around. Here's my card. Call 911, then call the station and ask for Captain Angelo. Tell him what happened and tell him I need him to smooth this over for me."

"You got it Lee. Are you sure your arm is okay?"

"Yeah. Do you have paper towels in the bathroom?"

"Yeah, sure."

"Will you get me three of them, and grab a roll of duct tape on your way back."

"Sure. But what…….? Never mind."

Grayson went to the bathroom and came back with three paper towels and a roll of duct tape.

"Here you go Lee."

"I'm going to need you to help me for a minute."

"Sure just let me know what you want me to do."

Detective Burton pulled up his sleeve and said, "Put those paper towels together and fold them in about a four inch by four inch square.

Grayson folded the paper towels.

"Okay now what?"

"Give 'em to me."

Detective Burton took the paper towels and put them over the newly opened gunshot wound.

"Now rip off about a foot strip of tape."

"Okay."

"Now tape that right around the middle of the paper towels."

Grayson ran the tape around the middle of the paper towels.

"Okay, that's really good. Now rip off two more pieces. Put one around the top and one around the bottom."

Grayson put a strip of tape around the top of the paper towels and one around the bottom.

"Okay that should hold it."

"Okay that's good. Real good. Thanks for your help."

Two minutes later.

Ring.

Ring.

Ring.

"Dammit," Detective Burton said.

"What's wrong Lee."

"Oh nothing. It's the little woman now."

"Hi Leann."

"Hi Lee. Are you okay?"

"Sure why wouldn't I be."

"I can hear you thinking. Remember?"

"Oh yeah. I know that. I just keep forgetting. But I'm okay. It was just a little incident. It's okay now. It's all over. I'll be home as soon as I can."

"Okay Lee. Be careful."

"Always Leann. I really have to go if I'm going to get everything done."

"Okay."

"Oh Leann."

"Yes."

"Tell Meaghan daddy says hi."

"Okay that's cute. I'll tell her. She should like that since she started it in the first place."

"Bye Leann."

"Bye Lee."

"Is everything okay Lee?" Grayson asked.

"Yeah, I think so. Leann is always bossin' me around and I'm not even having sex with her. I think I just got a dose of what it would be like to be married."

"Yeah."

"Aaahhh! This arm is killing me. I don't even know if I can get that trunk by myself."

"Hey look Lee, I'll go with you to get the trunk, and I didn't charge you for the truck this time."

"Nah, you have to charge me. My captain knows I'm coming over here for it. If you don't charge me for it they may accuse me of doing you a favor for the truck."

"Well, you kind of did."

"No. That was my job. Charge me for the truck. You can help me get the trunk in the house for nothing."

"Okay it's a deal."

"You sure drive a hard bargain kid," Detective Burton said smiling.

"Are you ready to go Lee?"

"Yeah. Oh dammit. I have to wash my arm off."

"Okay. Take your time."

"I'll only be a minute."

Detective Burton was back in three minutes and headed to the truck with Grayson.

"Wait a minute," Detective Burton said. "I have to get something out of my trunk and put it in the back of your truck.

Four minutes later.

"There that should do it. Let's go."

"I'll drive Lee."

"Thanks Grayson."

"But since I am going with you now, I'm going to run in and call 911 and your Captain Angelo."

"Great. Thanks."

Chapter 30

In twenty seven minutes Detective Burton and Grayson drove into the driveway of the safe house.

"Lee what the hell happened here?" Grayson yelled.

"Somebody tried to take us out," Detective Burton replied calmly. "You remember that cute girl Meaghan that I brought by your shop with Leann?"

"Yeah I remember."

"She is a witness against the Chicago mob and they hit the house trying to kill her. That means they tried to kill me and Leann too."

"So that's how you got shot in the arm?"

There was a long pause.

"No not exactly. It was a few days before that, when they hit the other safe house."

"Have you ever thought about getting into another line of work Lee?"

"It has crossed my mind a time or two."

"Yeah I'll bet."

"Hey Grayson. I think we should have some water in the refrigerator. You want one?"

"Sure. That would be good."

Detective Burton went to the refrigerator and got two bottles of water and gave one to Grayson.

"Thanks Lee."

"You're welcome."

"So I guess that little soiree back at the shop was a picnic compared to what you have been through the last couple of weeks."

"Yeah pretty much. Now let's get that trunk loaded and taken to the other new safe house so I can get home in time to eat with Leann and Meaghan, or Leann is going to kill me."

"Yeah, now you are really getting a dose of married life," Grayson joked.

Detective Burton and Grayson took a few minutes to drink their water.

Then they loaded up the trunk in the bed of the pickup and drove off to the new safe house on Pecos Road.

"All right there is one thing I have to tell you."

"What's that Lee?"

"I am taking you to the new safe house with me because I honestly don't think I can unload the trunk by myself. I trust you Grayson. But you cannot tell anyone else what we did, and do not tell anybody about the safe house."

"I would never do that Lee."

"I know you wouldn't. I just mean in casual talk. Nobody must know where we are. It means Meaghan's life, and Leann's and my life too."

"I get it Lee. I would never mention it to anyone."

"Okay, I just wanted to stress the importance of the secrecy. We have already been attacked twice."

"Okay Lee, your secret, it's safe with me."

"Good."

Chapter 31

Grayson backed the pickup into the driveway at Detective Burton's direction.

Detective Burton opened the garage door.

Grayson stopped the truck and got out.

"Hey Lee. I think I can unload the trunk by myself. I'll just drop it down a little bit at a time, right onto the two wheeler. Don't worry it will be okay. It's pretty strong. I know, I made it myself."

"Okay but if you think you need a hand, let me know. I've got one."

"Nah, I'll be okay."

Grayson jumped into the bed of the truck and untied the trunk. He pushed it onto the tailgate. Then he positioned the two wheeler just right and pulled the trunk to the edge of the tailgate. He spun the trunk around and let one end slide off onto the two wheeler. Then he pulled the other end upright onto the two wheeler.

"Good job," Detective Burton said. "Here is the key to the house. It should be that one right there. While you set the trunk in the master bedroom, I'll go set the camera and Claymores in place, and the Turf Builder."

"Okay."

Detective Burton set the camera in place and wired up one of the Claymore mines to the burner phone and put a bag of Turf Builder in front of it.

He heard footsteps crunching in the grass and a twig snap.

Detective Burton put his hand on his service weapon and quickly looked up.

"How is it going?" Grayson asked.

"Oh just great. I just have this one Claymore mine to wire up and we are ready to go."

Detective Burton shoved the legs of the last Claymore mine into the ground and wired it to the burner phone. He placed the bag of Turf Builder in front of it.

Then Detective Burton said to Grayson, "well I'm ready to go if you are."

"I'm ready."

"Good," Detective Burton replied. "Then by the time I get home it'll be time to change the paper towels and duct tape on my arm."

Grayson chuckled.

Detective Burton and Grayson got into the pickup and drove off to Grayson's Body Shop.

Chapter 32

Grayson drove the truck into one of the empty bays.

"Oh damn," Detective Burton groaned. "I'm sorry about all of this crime scene tape. But don't worry it shouldn't be up for long. They'll figure it out quick. It's a no-brainer."

"Don't worry about it Lee. Look on the bright side."

"There's a bright side."

"Yeah, with all of the news crews here, look at all of the free publicity I'm getting."

"Yeah, I guess there is a silver lining in just about everything. If you look hard enough for it."

"Yeah I guess."

"When I get home I'll type up a report on the incident here and email it to Captain Angelo."

"Thanks Lee."

"Well I'm going home," Detective Burton sighed. "I hope I didn't screw you up too bad."

"Hey, it could have been a whole lot worse if you hadn't been here."

"Yeah maybe. I'll see ya."

"Bye Lee."

Detective Lee Burton got into his dull red Charger, and headed for his apartment.

Chapter 33

Detective Burton pulled into his parking space. He locked the Charger and started out to his apartment. He knew it was only temporary, but he was glad to have someone to come home to.

Detective Burton walked up to the door of his apartment and put the key in the lock.

Then he thought. *Leann it's me. I'm coming in.*

He unlocked the door and started inside.

Meaghan jumped up from the table. She had a look of fear in her eyes when she looked at Detective Burton.

"Relax hon. It's only me."

"I didn't know Lee."

"I knew it was him Meaghan. I should have told you."

"How did you know? He didn't say anything."

"Well it is his apartment. Who else would it be with his own key?" Leann responded. "Nobody is going to find us here."

"Leann is right sweetie. We're safe here."

"Okay. I guess I'm just scared after the last few days we've had."

"I don't blame you for being scared Meaghan," Detective Burton told her. "But you don't have to be scared anymore. From now on Leann and I are both going to be with you."

"Thanks Lee. I feel a lot better knowing you're back."

"I do too Lee," Leann replied.

Then Detective Burton turned to face Leann, exposing his right arm to her.

"Lee why do you have duct tape on your arm?"

"I told you I would make it home in time to eat with you girls."

"Lee. Don't dodge me. Why do you have duct tape on your arm. Did you get shot again?"

"No."

"Then what?"

"I just opened the wound again. The one I already had."

"Didn't you go to Grayson's Body Shop to get a truck?"

"Yes I did."

Then Leann said, "Does it have anything to do with the news we saw this afternoon?"

"What news?"

"The news that said, lone cop foils a robbery at Grayson's Body Shop."

There was a long pause.

"Yeah, that was me."

"I figured."

"Leann it wasn't my fault. The guy was just there when I walked in. It's not like I go out looking for trouble."

"I know," Leann answered softly.

There was a long awkward pause from Detective Burton.

Then he finally said, "would you do something for me Leann?"

"Of course."

"I need a real bandage put on my arm. I have a first aid kit under my kitchen sink."

"I'm sure you do."

"It's the door on the end. Thanks."

Leann opened the door at the end of the counter and got the first aid kit.

"Come here," Leann ordered. "Sit here at the table."

"Okay."

"I'll clean that up for you first."

"Thanks. I'm sorry to put you through so much trouble."

"Don't even worry about it. It was a good thing you did Lee."

"Yeah, I thought so."

"You did."

"Yes I know. But they will still probably try to hang me out to dry."

"What does that even mean Lee?"

"It means they will try to punish me somehow."

"I don't think so Lee. Captain Angelo will not permit that to happen to you."

"Yeah, you're right Leann. It's good to have friends in high places, real high places."

"So how does that feel Lee?"

"Good. It feels good. Thank you."

"You're welcome, and I'm sorry. You had a rough enough time doing your good deed. Putting yourself in danger to help somebody else. Then when you came home I just made you feel worse."

"Don't worry about that. You're blending in very well Leann. That's what women do."

"I did not know."

"I know you didn't. You are the best partner I have ever had or ever will have. I'm so glad I got to know you."

"I am glad I got to know you too Lee."

"So are you girls cooking tonight?"

Then Leann said, "It's been a trying day Lee maybe we will just have something delivered."

"Sure, that works for me," Detective Burton mumbled. "I'm going to take some Ibuprofen. Maybe three or four."

"Just take two Lee. I don't want to have to call the suicide hot line for you."

"Well look who has a sense of humor. Where did that come from?"

"Is your arm still hurting you that bad?"

"Yes it is. Maybe you should have just made me bullet-proof like I asked."

"What are you two talking about?" Meaghan asked.

"Nothing hon. We're just kidding around," Detective Burton told her. "You want to order something to eat? You probably have the credit card number memorized by now."

"Actually I do."

"Okay then. Figure something out and get to it. After we eat do you want to try out one of those board games?"

"Yeah, sure," Meaghan answered excitedly.

Meaghan called the pizza place and decided on having a pepperoni pizza and three side salads.

Detective Burton was stocked up on Bud Light. He wasn't much of a drinker, but he did like to have a beer with pizza.

"Hey girls," Detective Burton said. "I am really tired. I'm going to take a fast bath."

"Bath?" Leann questioned. "I thought you were more of a shower man."

"I am. But I need to wash around this bandage."

"Oh yeah. Sorry."

"I'll see you girls in about twenty minutes or so. Here is some money for a tip."

"Thanks Lee," Meaghan replied.

Detective Burton went to take a bath and then returned to the living room. "I feel so much better," Detective Burton said with a sigh. "If you girls want to get cleaned up, I'll watch the fort."

"Yes I would like to get a nice hot bath," Leann replied.

"Yeah I would too," Meaghan said.

"Leann."

"Yes."

"Do you mind if we go in at the same time?" Meaghan asked. "So I can talk to you while you take your bath. Then you can talk to me while I take mine."

"Of course not sweetie. We can have some girl talk and maybe I can brush your hair when you get done."

"Cool Leann. I would really like that. My mom brushes my hair at home. I really miss that, and I miss my mom."

"Don't worry about anything. Lee and I will keep you safe and get you back home to your mom."

"I know you will," Meaghan told Leann.

Leann and Meaghan took their baths and came back out to the living room in about thirty five minutes.

"The pizza came while you girls were taking your baths and talking. I put it in the refrigerator. We can warm it up when you get ready to eat."

"I think we are ready. Right Leann?" Meaghan asked.

"Right. Let us warm it up."

"That's okay with me," Detective Burton said. "I was hungry an hour ago."

"Oh come on Lee. You are not going to starve," Leann replied laughing.

Then Detective Burton said, "I'll go warm up the pizza."

Detective Burton, Leann and Meaghan ate and talked and laughed. They enjoyed their meal and each other's company. And after they ate they played board games until midnight.

Then Detective Burton finally said, "Girls I really hate to put a damper on things, but I really am beat. My arm is hurting. I have to take some pills and go to bed."

"Only take two," Leann ordered.

"Okay. I got it."

NEXT MORNING AT THE SAFE HOUSE

Chapter 34

The next morning after having a big breakfast at the Village Inn in the Queen Creek Marketplace, Detective Burton drove the Charger into the driveway of the new safe house.

It was nine fifteen a.m.

"Girls this is going to be a lot better than before. Nobody but us knows where we are. We'll be fine here."

"Lee is right Meaghan. We really will be safe here."

"Hey girls, I saw a Del Taco on the way over here. How do you feel about tacos when it gets to be lunch time?"

"That would be great Lee," Meaghan replied.

"I don't know," Leann questioned.

"They have hamburger in 'em Leann," Detective Burton said, with a big smile.

"Okay tacos it is," Leann responded.

Detective Burton laughed.

"You know they even have hamburgers there, if you would rather have one."

"No, I will try tacos."

"Good. I'm going for a swim girls. When I came over here to set the house up I did some shopping. I got us a big beach ball."

"Oh that will be so cool Lee," Meaghan beamed. "If I only had a swimsuit."

"Don't worry; I've got you girls covered. Well almost. I stopped by Target and got a couple of bikinis. The girl working in that department said for the right size it is just a matter of pulling the strings a little tighter."

"Yeah that should work," Meaghan said.

"They're laying right on top of my suitcase."

"You think of everything Lee," Leann replied.

"Yes I do. At least I try."

Leann and Meaghan went into the bedroom and put their bikinis on and came back out by the pool where Detective Burton was waiting.

"I blew the beach ball up while you girls were changing. Now I'm going to put my trunks on. I'll be right back."

"I laid them out on the bed for you," Leann said.

"Okay thanks."

Detective Burton went into the bedroom and changed into his swimming trunks.

Then he got two Glock 19s from his suitcase. He wrapped them up in a towel. Both guns had a magazine with a fifteen round capacity. He knew they would be safe at the new house; he just couldn't bring himself to take any chances.

Detective Burton pulled out his iPhone 7 and dialed a restricted number.

Ring.

Ring.

Ring.

"Hello this is Tex."

"Tex it's Lee."

"Hey man, how the hell are you?"

"I'm fine Tex. I don't have a lot of time. I'm calling you on the sly. I need you and the guys to do me a favor."

"Sure Lee. Just name it."

"Actually you'll be doing the world a favor."

"Even better Lee," Tex said with a laugh.

"Listen Tex. I have a lot of things to tell you and a short time to talk. So I am going to send you an email later tonight. You have two weeks to hit seven targets. I have the addresses, the layouts and the floor plans for them all. Only hit the targets named and nobody else."

"Got it Lee," Tex answered. "I'll be waiting for your email."

"Thanks Tex. I think you'll do better on this job if you use the silent treatment."

"I understand Lee. I'll get the band together for our next gig."

"Thanks Tex."

Detective Burton ended his call to Tex and went back out by the pool.

The girls were already in the pool and throwing the ball to each other.

"Hey girls, you got room for me?"

"Yes there will always be room for you Lee," Leann answered.

Then she laughed and threw the ball to Meaghan.

Detective Burton jumped into the pool.

"Your bandage Lee," Leann yelled.

"Don't worry Leann. I'll change it later."

Chapter 35

For the next two weeks Detective Burton, Leann and Meaghan lived in the safe house on Pecos Road. They played cards, board games and played in the pool.

Then it was time for Meaghan to go back to Chicago to testify against the hitman she had seen kill a man in cold blood. Not to mention he had chased after her and tried to kill her while she was driving away to escape from him.

Detective Burton knew it was crucial for Meaghan to get back to Chicago safely. He did not want to trust the Chicago police for transport. So he had made arrangements with Captain Angelo to notify them that the transport would be handled on our end.

Detective Burton knew this was a job for the U.S. Marshals now. He knew a couple of U.S. Marshals from the Phoenix office. They were in the army with him and he trusted them to keep Meaghan safe.

Captain Angelo also arranged to have the two U.S. Marshals, who were Detective Burton's friends, to escort Meaghan back to Chicago. They would stay with her at all times until the trial was over.

They also got two more U.S. Marshals from the Chicago office on Dearborn Street to meet them at O'Hare Airport. The U.S. Marshals met them at the airport in a white van and took them to an undisclosed location until the trial started.

TWO WEEKS EARLIER

Chapter 36

Outside the City of Chicago in the city of Elmhurst, Illinois, four men in U.S. Army fatigues parked down the block from the biggest mob boss in the Chicago area.

They walked down to the house, each armed with an M-16, two Glock 19s with silencers and a crossbow. The men wore camouflage make-up. They scaled the wall of the ten million dollar house. Once on the other side of the wall, they used the oleanders for cover. Just like the plan said, four men with automatic rifles were standing in front of the house and four men were on the balcony of the second floor. The soldiers took out the four men on the ground first. There were four swishing sounds of the arrows leaving the crossbows. Four men dropped to the ground.

The soldiers raised their M-48 Kommando Automatic Crossbows and fired four more times, thrusting forth four more arrows at over one hundred and sixty feet per second. The other four guards went down.

The soldiers scaled the wall up to the balcony.

Inside the kingpin's office he was counting piles of money.

Combat boots quietly walked across the hardwood floor.

One of the soldiers walked up behind the ruthless kingpin.

A huge muscular arm wrapped around the kingpin's neck. The soldier pulled out his M9 Bayonet and shoved it through the kingpin's right temple and out through his left temple, causing instantaneous death.

The soldier pulled the bayonet back out, wiped the blood off on the kingpin's shirt and returned it to its sheath.

The soldier took a picture of the dead man with his cell phone camera.

Then he went down the hall.

He opened the door to a room and saw two little boys asleep.

The soldier closed the door quietly and walked down the hall to the next door.

He opened the door quietly. From the light of the night-light he saw a woman raise up in bed.

"Don't be afraid ma'am. I'm not going to hurt you. I checked on your kids. They're okay."

She turned on the bedside lamp as the soldier stepped closer to her.

"Did your husband do that to your face ma'am?"

"Yes."

"He won't ever hurt you again. I just killed him. I had to do it to save the life of a young girl that he wants killed. You should be safe now. My men and I are making six more stops in the next few days."

The soldier turned to leave. His hand had just reached the door knob.

"Wait," the woman called to him.

"Yes ma'am."

"Thank you."

The soldier left the bedroom and went back to the balcony.

He worked his way down the rope to the driveway. With the other soldiers in his squad, they scaled the wall in front of the house.

They returned to their car and drove off into the night.

Within the next six days they hit their other six targets with no collateral damage.

They took pictures of every man they killed, as proof of death. When the assignment was finished they mailed them all to TV stations ABC, CBS and WGN along with a letter that said this message.

We know these mob bosses are dead because we killed them. The cops can't stop us. The mob can't stop us. Nobody can stop us. We just proved that. If the rest of the mob stays in the Chicago area, they will die too.

DE OPPRESSO LIBRE.

PRESENT DAY

Chapter 37

The U.S. Marshals escorted Meaghan into the courtroom.

She looked like a very small child among these tall muscular men.

Every day the U.S. Marshals stayed close to Meaghan during the trial, at lunch breaks and at night in the safe house while she slept.

After two weeks the trial ended, with the conviction of the hitman Samuel Persefone, and as it turned out in order to ensure Meaghan's future safety key members of the Chicago mob were killed by a team of highly trained Special Forces soldiers.

The rest of the mob members saw the TV news broadcast about what had happened to key members of the mob and what would happen to any of them who remained in Chicago.

The remaining mob members booked flights out of Chicago.

The team of soldiers was now sure that Meaghan Foster would be safe.

These four Special Forces soldiers made up a very unique team known as Blackhawk. Their mission is always to eliminate any threat to the United States of America, on American or foreign soil.

Now that their mission was completed they would board their private jet at O'Hare Airport and fly home. The Blackhawk team answers only to the President of the United States.

But this time they were acting to help out a friend, who was once a member of the team.

Detective Lee Burton.

Chapter 38

Detective Lee Burton and Detective Leann Robins entered Detective Burton's apartment at six thirty six p.m.

They were done for the day.

"I sure am glad we stopped to eat," Detective Burton stated.

"Yes. I am too. They have great hamburgers at Texas Roadhouse."

"Yeah we should go there and try the steak some time."

"Yes we should Lee. The way you talk about it, I think I would really like it."

"I'm sure you would Leann, in about two or three days let's go get one."

"Okay. I would like to do that Lee. I like doing things with you."

"I like doing things with you too Leann."

"Good. I am glad."

Then Detective Burton said to Leann, "Hey would you like to get our showers and sit around and watch TV for a while?"

"Yes. I like to watch TV. Meaghan and I used to watch TV when you went out to fix up the safe houses."

"Oh that was nice."

"Yes it was."

"Okay you get a shower first and I'll make us some popcorn. I think you will enjoy it."

"Okay Lee, if you say so," Leann replied, as she went in to use the master bedroom shower.

Detective Burton went to the kitchen and got out a bag of popcorn and laid it on the counter.

In a few minutes Leann was back in the living room.

"Okay it's my turn now. When you hear the shower turn off, put that bag of popcorn in the microwave for a minute and forty five seconds."

"Okay I got it."

"I'll be quick."

"Wait Lee."

Detective Burton turned around to see what Leann wanted.

She walked up to him and hugged him.

"What was that for?"

"I just like you. Isn't that what people do when they like each other?"

"Yes. That is what people do. Thank you for hugging me. I needed that."

Detective Burton turned back around and went into the bedroom.

When Detective Burton showered and got dressed he splashed on some cologne so he would smell good. He knew nothing could ever happen between him and Leann; he just wanted to smell good for her.

Detective Burton went back out to the living room.

"That popcorn sure does smell good doesn't it?" Detective Burton asked.

"Yes it does," Leann agreed smiling. "And it tastes good too. I tried some while I was waiting for you."

"Well good. I'm glad you like it. What do you feel like watching on TV?"

Just then Detective Lee Burton's cell phone rang.

Ring.

Ring.

Ring.

"Detective Lee Burton speaking."

"Hi Lee," the cheerful voice on the other end said.

There was a long pause.

"Are you there Lee?"

"Yes. I'm here."

"It's me Meaghan."

"Oh hi Meaghan. You sound different on the phone."

"Yeah a lot of people tell me that."

"Hey Leann is right here. Can I put you on speaker?"

"Of course. I want to talk to her too."

"Okay you're on speaker hon."

"Hi Leann. How are you?"

"Hi Meaghan I am fine. How are you?"

"I'm great guys. The trial was over yesterday so I wanted to call and let you know how it went."

"Great," Detective Burton replied. "It must feel good to have the trial over."

"I am sure it does," Leann said. "How did it go for you?"

"They got a conviction on Samuel Persefone the hitman I was testifying against."

"That's great Meaghan," Detective Burton replied. "He will be in prison for the rest of his life. You won't have to worry about him anymore."

"Yes that is good news. But something weird happened."

"What do you mean Meaghan?" Leann asked.

"Well about two weeks before the trial started a group of soldiers attacked seven big mob bosses. They killed them all but never touched the women or children."

"It sounds like they were on a mission with no collateral damage. They knew exactly who their targets were. They knew the women and children were innocent," Detective Burton explained.

"Yes I guess," Leann commented.

Then Meaghan said, "the soldiers sent pictures of the dead guys to the local TV stations. They also sent a letter to the media. This is what they said. 'We know these mob bosses are dead because we killed them. The cops can't stop us. The mob can't stop us. Nobody can stop us. We just proved that. If the rest of the mob stays in the Chicago area, they will die too. De Oppresso Libre.'"

"Wow Meaghan," Detective Burton said. "These guys really mean business."

"Yeah they sure do," Meaghan replied. "It looks like I will be safe from the mob for sure now. I sure wouldn't want these guys after me."

"Yeah me neither," Detective Burton replied.

"What do you make of all this Lee?" Leann asked.

"Well, I do know enough to know that De Oppresso Libre is the motto of the United States Army Special Forces. It means liberate the oppressed."

"Well I guess that is what they sure did Lee," Meaghan responded.

"Yes it is, I sure am glad everything worked out so well for you Meaghan," Detective Burton told her.

"Yes me too," Leann added.

"Hey hold on a minute guys. My mom just came in. She had to work late. She wants to talk to you both. I'll put my phone on speaker."

"Hello detectives."

"Hello Mrs. Foster," Detective Burton and Leann said at the same time.

"Meaghan has talked about you two non-stop ever since she got back from Arizona. She thinks you two are the coolest things since ice cubes."

"We got pretty attached to Meaghan too," Detective Burton said. "She is a very good kid. I'm sorry; I guess I should say a very nice young lady. You must be very proud of her."

"Yes sir I am, and that is why I wanted to talk to you both. I wanted to make sure I said thank you for saving Meaghan's life for me. She is all I have. I missed her so much when she was out there in Arizona with you. Detective Burton, she said they call you Angel Cop. Now I know why she was so safe with you."

"Thank you Mrs. Foster. But you do know I'm not really an angel don't you? My partner Detective Robins is the real Angel Cop."

"Okay detectives, I won't keep you any longer. I just wanted a chance to thank you for everything you did for Meaghan."

"It was our pleasure Mrs. Foster."

"It sure was," Leann agreed. "I know how you felt when Meaghan was out here with us, because we miss her too."

"Yes ma'am," Detective Burton responded.

"Bye detectives."

"Bye Mrs. Foster," Leann said.

"Bye Mrs. Foster," Detective Burton said.

"Hey guys I'm still here!" Meaghan yelled. "I really should go too. Thank you for all you did while I was with you. I know you wouldn't have had to buy all of those games. You two are the best ones who ever protected me. I always felt safe with you. I love you guys."

"I love you too Meaghan."

"I love you too," Leann said. "I know we will all meet again someday."

"Bye guys."

"Bye hon," Detective Burton said.

"Bye sweetie," Leann replied.

Detective Burton and Leann looked at each other, as Detective Burton ended the call.

"Well Lee, now that we know Meaghan will be safe and get to fulfill her future; it is time for me to go home."

"But Leann it's still early."

"I know," Leann said sadly.

"Wait a minute Leann. You don't have a home. You live with me."

"I mean it is time for me to go back home, to heaven."

"Lucky you Leann."

"Yes I know."

"Will I see you again someday?"

"After living on earth for a while as a human, I have a lot more respect for you earth bound souls. Life on earth is hard Lee."

"Yes it is Leann."

Then Leann said to Detective Burton, "with all of the feelings and emotions you have to go through on a daily basis. All of the pain, suffering, sadness, sorrow, agony, injury and grief."

"But there are also good things too Leann. Things like love, joy, pleasure, satisfaction, delight and total bliss."

"Yes I know about joy. I have experienced joy too. It is mostly when I am with you Lee."

"I know I feel that too."

"Good," Leann replied. "I will stay here with you tonight Lee. But when you wake up in the morning, I will be gone. There is another soul waiting to lake my place in Leann's body. Captain Angelo will make sure that Leann is transferred to California. I guess I should say Gabriel the Archangel. I think you figured that out a while back. He trusted you Lee. He just wanted to be here too. He is the protector of children. The new soul will trade places with me when Leann is transferred to Los Angeles."

"That figures. The City of Angels."

"Maybe at one time," Leann whispered.

"Yeah maybe at one time," Detective Burton echoed.

Then Leann told Detective Burton, "The new soul will be a detective in Los Angeles. Her name will still be Leann Robins."

"Will she remember me?"

"No. She will not Lee."

"I'm going to miss you Leann."

"I will miss you too Lee. But we both knew this was just temporary."

"I know Leann. But it doesn't make it any easier."

"I know it does not. Hey there is something I would like to do."

"Sure anything Leann. Just ask."

"I checked already and it is okay for me to do. I would like to experience a kiss with a man. Would you kiss me Lee?"

"Sure, like I said, anything for you Leann."

Detective Burton put his arms around her and pulled her close to him.

She put her arms around him too.

He leaned down and pressed his lips to Leann's soft warm lips.

He kissed her for a few seconds. When he pulled away Leann was looking right into his eyes. After a while she got a shocked look on her face.

Then Leann said, "Lee there is something wrong with my earth body."

"What is it? What's wrong Leann?"

"My stomach feels strange and my legs are getting weak."

Detective Burton laughed.

"Come over here and sit down on the couch for a while."

"What is wrong with me Lee?"

"There is nothing wrong with you. I feel the same way too. It means I did my job right. It is the way you are supposed to feel when you kiss someone you love or care a lot about. I'm glad I was able to do that for you Leann."

"Yes I enjoyed that," Leann told Detective Burton. "I hope you enjoy the rest of your life Lee. It will be forever you know."

"Yes I do know."

"Life on earth is hard Lee. Do not spend the rest of your earth life alone. There is someone out there for you. She is an

258

old soul like you. She will love you and make you very happy. You deserve that Lee. You are a good man. Any earth woman would be lucky to have you for her man."

Then Leann looked into Detective Burton's eyes and said, "I will see you again Lee."

Chapter 39

The next morning Detective Lee Burton got up and went into Leann's bedroom.

She was gone.

A tear rolled down his cheek.

After a few minutes he went back to his bedroom and shaved and showered.

Then he went out and got into the Charger and drove off to the station.

It was seven forty five a.m. when he pulled into the station's parking lot.

Detective Burton walked into Captain Moore's office.

"Hey Lee. Come on in," the captain said.

"Good morning it's good to have you back Rick."

"It's good to be back Lee. Ya know I got word of Detective Robins' transfer but I have never found out where Captain Angelo came in from. I haven't found out where he went to either."

"Yeah I checked him out to Rick. I couldn't find a trace of him anywhere. It's probably just a records error. It happens all the time. I wouldn't worry about it anymore."

"Yeah I'm sure that's what it is too," Captain Moore replied.

"Well he seemed all right," Detective Burton commented. "Everybody liked him."

"Yes and I've been hearing a lot of great things about what Detective Robins did, helping you out on the Meaghan Foster case."

"Yeah she was great."

"I heard she saved your life."

"Yes she sure did."

"I was going to email a letter to her captain to let him know what a good job she did for us. But with no record of him

I couldn't do that. But I heard she was transferred to California, Los Angeles to be exact."

"Yeah, the City of Angels," Detective Burton commented.

"I guess I'll have to email it to her new captain out there."

"Yeah that would be nice captain."

Then Detective Burton thought.

And since that Leann is not the same soul, I'm sure that email will get lost somewhere in heaven.

"Well Lee, I wish I could have made it back a couple of days sooner so I could have met Detective Robins. She sounds like a remarkable woman."

"She sure is Rick. I really wish you could have met her too. I'm sure she made a big difference in everybody's life she met. I'm sure she changed it for the better."

"Except for Detective Ryan," Captain Moore remarked. "But she had to shoot him. There was no other choice. Right?"

"Right Rick. If she hadn't shot him, I'd be dead right now.......again."

"Yeah about that Lee. The guys have been telling me that you are different since you died and came back."

"Trust me Rick. That will do it for you."

"What I meant is I didn't think it was possible for you to put any more effort into you job than you already were. But the guys tell me you are even more committed than you were before. Why do you think that is?"

"Well Rick, I guess it's because I have finally figured it out."

"What's that Lee?"

"I'm doing God's work."

AUTHOR'S NOTE

I would like to explain the choosing of the names of characters in this book. I always try to think of names for my characters that are different and unique but not silly. I wanted to make the names in this book special and something that reflected on the characters themselves, especially the angel that Detective Lee Burton meets in heaven. Somehow my thoughts went to my two cousins Leann and Robin. I used both of their names for my angel character.

This is why I think Leann Robins is the perfect name for the angel.

Urban dictionary definition for Leann.

266

The name Leann means: an angel; one of sheer perfection; perfection personified; unrivaled beauty; one having a commanding presence. One devoid of flaws. The most magnificent creature crafted by God. Leann is not just perfect; she is an angel.

Definition of Robin:

The name Robin means, in spiritual meaning: transformation, growth, renewal, passion, change and power. Robin is all about perseverance and trying to "keep on keeping on." Robin has passion and this can be a sign of spiritually.

Meaghan Foster:

Meaghan in this particular spelling I chose means: Pearl and is of American origin. A pearl is also a gem, a precious stone.

The last name Foster is an ancient name meaning "guardian of the forest." In this case the forest was the people of Chicago she chose to protect by going up against the Chicago mob.

Detective Lee Burton:

Lee: In the United Kingdom the name Lee means "Gift of God." Since he was shot and died and was returned to earth alive, that makes him a gift of God.

Burton: From a surname that was originally taken from an old English place name meaning "fortified town." This also fit very well because Detective Lee Burton was always fortifying the safe houses to better protect Meaghan. I also hope you caught that he felt like he also had to protect Leann as well because she did not have all of her angel powers.

The Hitman Samuel Persephone:

The name Persephone means: "bringer of death and destruction" and is of Greek origin.

Captain Gabriel Angelo:

Turned out to be Gabriel the Archangel, protector of children. Since Meaghan was not yet eighteen years old, she was still a child.

So now you have my thinking on the names I chose for my main characters of this book.

I also hope you caught all of the references to Leann being an angel and the references to expose Captain Gabriel Angelo's real identity.

I hope you enjoyed this book.

Happy reading.

DLR

About the Author

Now retired Donald L. Rost lives in the San Tan Valley in Arizona. He now spends his time writing and being with his grandson as often as possible. He is a Vietnam Veteran who served in 1969 through 1970. Included in his medals are an Army Commendation Medal and two Bronze Stars. He formerly worked at the Arizona State House of Representatives in security and worked close with law enforcement officers in providing protection for politicians and state workers.

www.ingramcontent.com/pod-product-compliance
Lightning Source LLC
Chambersburg PA
CBHW070321260626

47160CB00003B/913